FUTUREWAYS

EDITED BY RITA MCBRIDE
& GLEN RUBSAMEN

Arsenal Pulp Press, Vancouver
Whitney Museum of American Art, New York
Printed Matter, Inc., New York

FUTUREWAYS

Alexandre Melo's text translated from the Portuguese by Brad Cherry

Cover and interior design by David Gray
Cover photograph of Leonard Nimoy viewing Joseph Beuys's *Enterprise 11/18/72, 18:5:16 hours* (*Enterprise 18.11.72, 18:5:16 Uhr*), 1973, by Michael Sandler.

Printed and bound in Canada

Library and Archives Canada
Cataloguing in Publication
Futureways / edited by Rita McBride and Glen Rubsamen.
(Ways book)
Co-published by: Whitney Museum of American Art, Printed Matter, Inc.
ISBN 1-55152-172-5
I. McBride, Rita, 1960- II. Rubsamen, Glen
III. Printed Matter, Inc. IV. Whitney Museum of American Art. V. Series.
PS8600.F87 2004 C813'.6 C2004-902949-5

This project is a copublication between Arsenal Pulp Press, the Whitney Museum of American Art, and Printed Matter, Inc.

ARSENAL PULP PRESS
103 – 1014 Homer Street, Vancouver, BC, V6B 2W9, Canada
arsenalpulp.com
Arsenal Pulp Press is one of North America's leading independent publishing houses.

WHITNEY MUSEUM OF AMERICAN ART
945 Madison Avenue, New York, NY 10021, USA
whitney.org
The Whitney Museum of American Art is the leading institution of twentieth- and twenty-first century American art and culture. An essential forum for American artists since its founding in 1930, the Whitney's goal is to champion freedom of artistic expression and to foster the development of art in America.

PRINTED MATTER, INC.
535 West 22nd Street, New York, NY 10011, USA
printedmatter.org
Printed Matter, Inc. is an independent 501(c)(3) non-profit organization founded in 1976 by artists and art workers with the mission to foster the appreciation, dissemination, and understanding of artists' books and other artists' publications.

ARSENAL PULP PRESS WHITNEY Whitney Museum of American Art Printed Matter, Inc.

Contents

THE FUTURE LASTS A LONG TIME

YING ZONG 4217*

Before I proceed with my testimony regarding the Events of 2199, I must address the rumors about myself that have been circulating in the world media: necessarily I am compelled to confirm these rumors. I am indeed one of the seventeen members of Mission Impossible 2175. Given that so many of my colleagues' memoirs and other writings about the assignment have already been made public, and given that I am the only member remaining on Earth, I see no reason to hide this facet of my identity any longer, especially now that it has become a matter of public speculation, and one of seemingly relevant concern to this court. Although I have no new insights or details to add to the accounts already given by my colleagues regarding the success of Mission Impossible 2175, I shall take the liberty here to confirm this aspect of my past as evidence that I am not currently on Earth of my own volition, or due to my own merit. I hope this piece of personal history will further bolster my plea before the court that I took no part in the Manhattan Uprising of 2199.

I was forced into servitude on Mission Impossible 2175 because of egregious errors committed during my

**Formerly known as the art critic Laura Cottingham.*

last life. Actually, there was only one egregious error, specifically one German bitch, who caused my downfall. To those of you who might feign shock that an international art critic such as myself should have played any part in Mission Impossible 2175 – "Where did you find the time?" is the question most likely to be put to me – I recommend that you review the life accomplishments of the other sixteen members of that assignment; you will find that each of us sustained some kind of earthly career in addition to the Mission. My career as an art critic is no more or less ordinary, or distinctive, than those earthly roles occupied by the research biotechnicians, yoga teachers, video actresses, dithyrambic plumbers, and other professionals who filled our ranks. After all, on Earth one is forced to do something.

On my last return I had been off Earth for so long that whole new continents had been created, so it wasn't really my fault that I returned to an inopportune location. Or at least I didn't blame myself at the time. Now, I am not so sure. When I was here in the twentieth century, I reasonably concluded that my reappearance in a small town in the southern United States was the result of my own negligence in keeping abreast of the affairs on Earth that had occurred in my absence. It was for that reason that I mistimed or mislocated – depending on whether you prefer to speak in terms of time or space, although personally I regard such distinctions rather useless – my re-entry.

I am certain that during the twentieth century when I asked for Paris, I was quite ignorant of the fact that a new Earthly principality had emerged with the legal right to use all the names of previous centuries and Earthly civilizations and stick them anywhere willy-nilly. Who could have imagined that there would emerge such people who would apply the term "Paris" to any old piece of dirt and grass that might be around? Admittedly, if I hadn't spent my time whiling away the centuries in the Land of the Lotus Eaters I might have known, as others obviously did, that the eighteenth century had ushered in a new empire that by the twentieth century had no less than fifteen cities all called Paris. Still, that little error really fucked me up. For the first decade of that existence most of my energies were spent on the redundant task of just trying to figure out where I was! At the age of two, when I had absorbed enough of the American language to speak it with halting fluency, I began to protest my location, adamantly denying that wherever I was, it wasn't Paris. My elders completely misunderstood my confusion and insisted, against my violent verbal and physical protests to the contrary, that we were indeed living in Paris. It wasn't until my seventh or eighth year, when the information available to me through reading *Encyclopaedia Britannica* provided me with the knowledge I had been lacking. I finally realized that the mistake was mine: I had asked for Paris, not knowing that such a request needed to be more specific to accommodate the new continents and new locations with old names that now existed on twentieth-century Earth.

Ashamed as I am, I must admit that with this, my current and twenty-second-century arrival, I wasn't even given a choice of location. Given that my status upon arrival was so low, I plead the court to reconsider the charges against me, especially given that my low status is evidence in and of itself that I do not and have never possessed in this lifetime the powers that are being attributed to me, powers that would absolutely have been necessary to the leading participants of the Manhattan Uprising of 2199, in which, I assert again before the court, I was neither complicit nor an active participant.

In regard to the Events of 2199 it is well established that I was at the Shanghai Biennial that year, during Lunar Months Five and Six. I participated as a guest curator. Why my name continues to figure in the List of Potentially Seditious in New York given all the records that testify to my activities in Shanghai baffles me. For those unconvinced of the reliability of passport and trans-jet documents, both of which have already been produced and are in the hands of this court, I offer as additional evidence the front page of the *Shanghai Express*, which features a photograph of me in the main gallery of the Neue Artistes Musée taken on Lunar Month Five, 21, 2199, the day before the Manhattan Uprising. My treatment at the Soma Clinic of Shanghai from Month Five, 21–27, is also a matter of public record and has been duly submitted before the court.

I should perhaps confess here that I am flattered by the court's belief in my talent. But the suggestion that I am capable of instantaneous travel or coterminous presence is nothing more than flattery, as I assure the court that I am not advanced enough to access either of those powers! My affiliation with Mission Impossible 2175 should be testament enough to the level of life I am capable of obtaining. If any of us were advanced enough to accomplish either instantaneous travel or coterminous presence we would not have been drafted on Mission Impossible 2175, which, as I have already stated, is evidence in and of itself of low birth and limited power. As my preamble to this testimony makes clear, I am not a miscreant! I am not a heathen! I accept the Laws of the universe and am trying my best to obey them!

The Laws, as all of you well know, do not allow such advanced powers as instantaneous travel and coterminous presence to those of us who have not advanced past the purple sphere. I call your attention to the recent volume published by Professor Kathe Burkehardt, *The Chakra Energies Aboard Mission Impossible* 2175, wherein the professor gives a detailed account of the Karmic positions of all members of that assignment and concludes that no members were likely to be higher than the emerald level. Having known all my colleagues on Mission Impossible 2175, I must agree with her assessment. The spectacular nature of our success was not the result of our great individual capacities but rather an event dictated by Karmic Law and which we were merely assigned to accomplish. As is well known, human action is necessary for human events to occur. I believe that Master Astronomer G. R. Denizen has made this case clear in his *Success and Mission Impossible* 2175, which includes irrefutable cosmic charts on each of the members of that Mission along with Denizen's own brilliant insights. I realize that my singular position as the only member of Mission Impossible 2175 left on Earth has given some reason to suspect me of possessing superior powers, but I would like to suggest that my situation could just as easily be viewed from the opposite perspective, i.e., that I am the last remaining Mission member on Earth due to failures rather than triumphs on my part! I should also like to remind the court that on Earth the human life span is variable and consequently some of us remain longer than others.

Given the confusion that remains with regard to my life during Lunar Month Five, 2199, I would like to recall for the court a detailed account of my activities and thoughts when the Manhattan Uprising occurred and I was in Shanghai. Before I begin I would like to assert that my lack of participation in the Manhattan Uprising should not be taken as either a negative or affirmative stance in regard to that event, but simply as testimony and evidence that I was not there.

I arrived in Shanghai on Lunar Month Five, 10, 2199, and used the days before the opening of the exhibition to co-ordinate the production of new artworks and install other historical works. I should perhaps give some account about the central premise of my Shanghai exhibition because I realize that my ideas themselves are to a large extent responsible for my inclusion on the List of Potentially Seditious in New York. I do not wish to claim a distinction between thought and action here because I believe that ideas and actions are indeed categorically continuous; rather, I wish to assert that my ideas do not in any direct way relate to the Manhattan Uprising. In addition to taking the necessary legal action to demonstrate that I was not present at the Manhattan Uprising, I would also like to illustrate more fully the nature of my ideas and therefore make obvious their absolute distinction from those ideas that laid the foundations for the Manhattan Uprising. Since the premise of my exhibition in Shanghai is considered suspect, I will begin with that. I also recommend to the court my essay in the catalog that accompanied the exhibition, which is available in a wide variety of multilinguistic formats, under the global exhibition title "The Future is Now."

THE FUTURE LASTS A LONG TIME

My exhibition, titled "The Future Lasts a Long Time," was based on two art exhibitions I curated on Earth at the end of the last millennium, in 1996 in what was then known as Denmark, and in 1997 in what was then known as France. Both of these locations were nations on the landmass known during the twentieth century as Europe. Yong Ling de Ling is now what was once known as Denmark. France, as everyone knows, no longer exists at all. These twentieth-century art exhibitions in Denmark and France were organized during my last incarnation when I was a citizen of the United States, but due to the political circumstances at that time, was forced to conduct my work in other nation states. Both of these exhibitions are historically documented in the World Library of Art and, had I chosen to announce my exhibition as one comprised of historical re-enactments, it would have been under a nomenclature so traditional in the conventions of artistic distribution as to arouse no controversy whatsoever. The convention which I am guilty of breaking is that I stated that the exhibitions belonged to a self I no longer legally or otherwise claim, to a self which Earth claims no longer exists. Despite the fact that I am not alone in my belief in time travel through rebirth, I acknowledge that few people are permitted to confess this belief publicly, and I knew at the time that I was taking an enormous risk in publicly proclaiming myself as one who has lived before, indeed, as one who was previously also a critic of contemporary art.

I should remind the court that my position is distinct in that no one had previously claimed to be the art critic formerly known as Laura Cottingham and, in fact, few had even heard of such a person until I emerged with my thesis. I should also remind the court that my position is devoid of any mercurial or legal claims to any kinds of property, intellectual or otherwise, belonging to the deceased – I was so constantly screwed over by publishers and the like in my past life that I would never consider for a moment trying to recover what was stolen from me two centuries ago!

The concept behind "The Future Lasts a Long Time" was to present as many works as possible from "Incandescent," the 1996 exhibition in Denmark, and "Vraiment: Féminisme et Art," organized for Le Magasin in Grenoble, France, in 1997. Although the concept of time travel through rebirth is implicit in the sense that I personally claimed to be redoing what I had, in another lifetime, already done, other, more conventional aspects of intellectual scholarship and art history were also embedded in this curatorial project. There is the question, of course, of the effect of history on the work of art. Which artworks last for one hundred or more Earth years and why? In addition to the superficial, but nonetheless intriguing, question of the mere physical preservation of the artwork, there is also the question of how time alters the perception of the artwork simply because time alters the perception of the audience. Even when time and governments are generous to the preservation of the art object, even when the physical properties of its medium are conserved to the greatest possible degree, an artwork can still appear meaningless to subsequent audiences! It took me over five years to track down with relative accuracy the fates that met the seventy-three artworks that had together comprised the two twentieth-century

European contemporary art museum exhibitions organized by the art critic formerly known as Laura Cottingham – you may speak of myself simply as an historical entity if my identification with this subjectivity disturbs you. Of the seventy-three items in question, only twenty-one were available for display in Shanghai. Of the fifty-two not available, thirty-seven can be said to no longer exist in any form, nine are of unknown whereabouts and possibly also extinct, and the other six are still extant but for various reasons were not available for Shanghai.

Although today it is well known that the artistic contributions which are most likely to endure through time are those created without tangible form – words, dance, and music – the twentieth century was the last century to believe absolutely in the permanence of objects. It is for this reason that the great art historian Anna Christmas Chavez refers to the twentieth century as "the Century of Grasping." The primitive beliefs that controlled the production, distribution, and evaluation of twentieth-century art products – especially in what was then referred to as "the West" – prioritized artistic efforts that found their expression as objects. Indeed, this false hope for permanence was accompanied by an egregious fetish for materials considered permanent. This misguided mania continued in dominant art centers such as New York even after the Act of God of September 11, 2001, when the spontaneous combustion of two towers was witnessed around the world and one might have thought, as Professor Tomasia Mackilvesky has observed, that nothing man makes can last forever. Indeed, as Mackilvesky's great research attests, the Act of God of September 11,

2001, apparently produced the opposite response among artistic practitioners and arts professionals who redoubled their investments in things, things, and more things.

Because of what we know now, it is especially interesting to reflect upon the actual life span of individual artworks produced at the end of the twentieth century. The twenty-one twentieth-century works exhibited in "The Future Lasts a Long Time" were presented alongside the results of my research into the fates that met all of the art presented in "Incandescent," 1996, and "Vraiment," 1997. The twenty-one works presented included works in all twentieth-century media: photography, oil painting, various objects, video, and film. The conservateur's reports on specific works is included verbatim in the exhibition catalog so I will not duplicate her efforts here; suffice to say that we found absolutely no correlation between physical materials and longevity in regard to the extended life of the artwork. Oil paintings composed from the same tubes of paint in the same artist's studio during identical years did not survive the same length of time! Materials considered fugitive and otherwise not lasting when they were produced during the twentieth century were just as likely to live into the twenty-second century. I will refrain from speculating here on the causes or reasons for this and suggest that those of you wishing additional documentation and insights into this phenomenon consult the most recent work by Kristina Stilesjo, *Motivation and Longevity in the Ephemera of Plasticity*.

The contemporary artists featured in "The Future Lasts a Long Time" were also drawn from my personal history and research into the art of the late twentieth century: I selected living artists who had had previous incarnations as artists I considered interesting at the end of the last millennium. As has been widely documented in the press, some of these artists claim not to have been the artists I consider them to be. This disagreement does not disturb me in the least; everyone is entitled to believe about himself or herself what they can and will. Still, I have complete faith in the psychic Tishon Muhammad, who assisted me in my research to locate the artists formerly known in the twentieth century as Alex Bag, Prince, Jack Goldstein, Elvis Presley, Cady Noland, Dennis Balk, Marianne Faithfull, Tony Feher, Leslie Singer, Al Pacino, Natacha Lesueur, Chuck Nanney, and Bruno Pelassy. There were a few other artists I wanted whom we couldn't find anywhere, but that's Earth life.

The Manhattan Uprising occurred between World Time 5:10 and 7:22 on Lunar Month Five, 22, 2199 – the day before the opening of my exhibition for the Shanghai Biennial. In keeping with the requests of the court, I will herewith attempt to reconstruct my activities during that time. I remind the court that 5:10 World Time occurs in Shanghai at the end of the afternoon, just before dusk. The sun sets in Shanghai during Lunar Month Five at approximately World Time 8:00.

On Lunar Month Five, 21, 2199, I spent the afternoon in the main galleries of the Neue Artistes Musée. By lunchtime all of the new installations by living artists had been completed and most of the artists left the Musée to take Soma in preparation for the opening. I continued to work with the preparateurs. Most of our work was concerned with spellchecking the wall labels. Shanghai adopted Euroenglish as its official language as recently as

2195; I was the only native Euroenglish speaker on the project. At about 3:00 World Time a member of the Musée's Shipping Department came into the galleries and informed me that an art shipment from Jing-Ling had arrived and required my signature. I told him that this was impossible, that I was not awaiting any art shipments from Jing-Ling or anywhere else. He insisted that World Fine Shipments had arrived with a crate and that the paperwork had already been cleared by the Musée's security system and they had verified my fingerprints encoded in the digital request system. I left the galleries to attend to this mystery.

When the crate was opened it was revealed to contain a single work of art by the twentieth-century American artist Adrian Piper. The work is composed of charcoal on paper, a drawing from 1981 titled "Self-Portrait Exaggerating My Negroid Features." Although Adrian Piper was one of the artists featured in "Incandescent," 1996, and "Vraiment," 1997, this work was not among those to be included in "The Future Lasts a Long Time." I had no idea why it was delivered to me, or even where it had come from. Subsequent investigation by the Musée has revealed that the shipping address in Jing-Ling refers to a place that does not exist; this case is still pending.

I picked up the self-portrait to examine it more closely. Indeed, it was as if I was drawn to it, or rather coerced toward it, by an invisible force. As I held the work in both hands, I underwent a singular and bizarre transformation that is image-documented – see Exhibit x42. Because of the emphatically strange response I had to this artwork, members of the Shipping Department immediately sent for a laser recorder to register the phenomenon. The image reveals what I looked like and I will try to explain here what I felt.

Mentally, I experienced a Trans-historical Flashback – although I had no term for the experience at the time. But as I looked at the artwork, which, as its title asserts, is a self-portrait, I experienced a distinct recollection of having experienced it before. As if struck by lightning, I suddenly remembered that this very same artwork was sent to me in 1997 in Grenoble – also by "accident" – from an art warehouse in New York, during the installation of "Vraiment." When this event took place in 1997 it was quite a trauma because I didn't know what to do. Le Magasin, Grenoble, where I was working as a guest curator, was under the directorship of a Satanic thief, and I feared trusting the museum with an undocumented piece because I knew the director was quite capable of either stealing or destroying the work (he had already stolen things from myself and others). I was hesitant at first to contact the artist to inform her of this error because such information could only serve to cause her anxiety and pain. I considered carrying the artwork back to New York with me and delivering it to the artist personally, but my travel plans included extended time in France and I didn't think I should journey with an artwork to the beach – and what if it were taken from me by customs at a border crossing? After much anxiety I finally contacted the artist directly. She was rightfully horrified but was eventually able to provide me with reasonable instructions that resulted in the work being returned, without further incident. The rather bizarre and unfortunate journey of "Self-Portrait Exaggerating My

Negroid Features," 1981, that occurred in the summer of 1997 was ironically and coincidentally brought back to me just a few short years later, in 2002. This very work – this piece of art so neglected as to have been thrown into a crate to be shipped across the Atlantic as if it were a banana peel tossed into a public dumpster – was chosen to blaze across the cover of the catalog for the artist's New York retrospective in 2002. Thinking back now, after everything that has happened – in the twentieth century as well as in our own – it is obvious that this image likes to travel.

On that fateful day of Lunar Month Five, 21, 2199, seeing this image again, holding it in my hands, all of my troubled and confused past experiences with this artwork tumbled into my psyche. While undergoing this trauma of the mind as I stood before that crate in the Musée's Shipping Department, my body began to morph back into its twentieth-century form. My chestnut skin, which you see before you today, turned pale. My thick black hair lost its strength and luster and turned golden brown. And much to the astonishment of the amazed onlookers in the Shanghai Neue Artistes Musée's Shipping Department, my body morphed into what was known in the late twentieth century as a "born-female."

Fortunately, the advanced treatments available to me from the Shanghai BioRegistration Committee on Human Formology have been successful and I have experienced no subsequent Fallbacks or Flashbacks. Indeed, after they were able to disengage me from the Adrian Piper drawing, my body form readjusted immediately. After a week of Soma treatments and LingPow aromas at the Double Happiness Temple, I regained peace of mind.

The Past-Life Survival Specialists who treated me in Shanghai will testify later today in regard to my condition between the hours of 5:10 and 7:22, when I was unconscious from Soma and under strict medical observation. The court can now see that my position at the time of the Manhattan Uprising is so well documented that it absolutely refutes any possibility that I was involved in any way. I herewith beg the court to remove my name from the List of Potentially Seditious in New York in order that I may continue my activities on Earth as long as I shall remain here.

THE CURATOR AWAKES

There was a pause on the line, which Jib Myers registered as a point of weakness in the argument. "I need to talk to the curator," he repeated, the urgency in his voice ratcheting up several notches and carrying with it the scent of because-I'm-important, because-I'm-busy, because-it's-my-right, as well as several other unintentional speech effects which were by no means lost on the administrator fielding this, Jib's third call in two days. For her part Maryam Hersh'l was privately as exasperated and nervous as Jib. And with good reason. His call was only one of a clutch of requests flowing in from artists, press, board members, and donors, both corporate and civic, for some portion of the curator's attention. Maryam had spent the last nine days bouncing them back – apologizing, excusing, and otherwise attempting, not entirely successfully, to bridge the gap between what the owners, members, writers, and donors wanted and what the curator seemed inclined to provide. She thought back to her first weeks, all those years ago at the Colorado Gymnasium of Applied Cultures, taking her major in cultural delivery systems. She recalled the text above the faculty entrance, which looped and rotated through its allegedly infinite variations – though this was hotly disputed by some members of the faculty who claimed that:

I) its variations were well short of "infinite" as they understood the term, and,

II) Applied Cultures had no damn business outsourcing its algorithmic requisitions to a rival faculty (in this case Iowa).

It was a nasty and, Maryam had felt, rather arcane debate – either way the colors did change a lot. And the memory of lovely Professor Bakr beaming out at them through his beard in the inaugural week saying, "See that sign, ladies and gentlemen? See those words? Read them, commit them to memory – let them be your creed from this day forth!" And how those words nibbled at her conscience now. Shifting form, color, texture, opacity, luminosity, and smell – but always making for an identical reading: "Doers, do. Writers, write. Owners, own, and Administrators *bridge the gap*."

This past week she hadn't felt like much of a gap-bridger. Instead she offered, "I'm sorry, Jib, but you can't speak to the curator right now." And now it was Jib's turn to pause, midway between crumpled and exasperated. Front it as he might, there was no way he was going to push his luck with Maryam Hersh'l.

He sighed. "Look, Maryam, I'm driving the work over to the pavilion as we speak. I'll be with you in about four hours."

"You're driving it yourself?" she asked.

"Yeah," replied Jib, his turn to go on the defensive at that implied slight. *I'm skimming, damn it, I'm skimming, and she knows I'm skimming.* And then to Maryam, "Yeah,

I didn't want to trust it to the transporters – you know it's a very important piece. . . ."

"Well, you know, Jib, they're really very good. . . ."

This was going terribly. *I ring up to complain about not being able to get an answer from that motherfucking gimmick of a curator /// and now I'm making Myers feel bad – shit, I'm making him feel bad – third law, girl, third goddamn law.* Professor Bakr again, beardy and wise – why was he in her thoughts so much these days? "Blame, ladies and gentlemen, blame. Don't take it and don't give it. Absorb it, reduce it, transpose it into something better."

"Well, it's brilliant you're taking the lead on that, Jib – not everyone would." *How was that for a recovery? Too patronizing? And for God's sake, what is Jib Myers of all people doing skimming the transport budget?*

"Yeah, yeah, that's what I was thinking," he replied, mollified, at least in part. A cough. Then an assertion. "So look, I'll be with you in four hours and I'd really appreciate it if I could talk briefly to the curator about placing the work. I've got no problem with the descriptors, but I'd really like to get the placement – well, I just wanna talk about it."

And now the honey, sweet and healing. "Of course, Jib. Of course. We've got a lot of people here working on it. Look forward to seeing you soon." They hung up.

Inside his vehicle (well, strictly speaking, vehicles) Jib relaxed and adjusted his genitals, scratched his ear, picked his nose, bit his bottom lip, and furrowed his brow a little. He let the post-adrenaline dip take hold (as though he could prevent it!), watched the clouds and mountains gliding by, and chided himself for his earlier welling-up of prejudice. He wasn't one of those racist bastards who hated the Materials. Sure, it presented all kinds of challenges and made you question all kinds of assumptions. But in a way one of the most positive things you could say about a Material Being was that it made you fundamentally question what it means to be human. Material Beings have been in the world for only fifteen years. The first one, called, rather predictably Jib had always thought, "Adam" by its creators at Material Life Sciences, had long been promised. Despite its creaking acronym – Artificial Dialogic Anthropomorphic Mechanism – Adam, the world's first fully sentient machine, had been a global *cause célèbre* and the generic name "Material Being" had been quickly attached to it. Some commentators of a pedantic mind-frame had pointed out that all life-forms were made up of material, either organic or non-organic, and were therefore, strictly speaking, Material Beings. The terms "non-organic beings" or "non-organic material beings" (or NOBS or NOMBS) had been advanced and, by that peculiar process by which a neologism succeeds or fails to enter the realm of nomenclature, had been rejected. Thus at the particular moment in history when Jib Myers was enjoying a slight increase in the speed of his convoy, the 300 or so sentient networks, artificial life forms, thinking/talking strings (or whatever their developers called them) were, at least in the popular imagination, called Material Beings.

The marketing screen to the left of Jib's lounge flickered back into life, indicating that his convoy had entered another commercial jurisdiction and, for the next fifteen minutes, he would be subjected to a mélange of short-burst financial expenditure options. He turned the sound down as far as it would go (i.e., "Low" – he was hauling an ORVIGO9000 series convoy and as these were part-owned there was no "Off" for the marketing sound). The cheery, cod-sensual voices of the Ad people commenced their routine burrowing into his brain. Jib had never much cared for the Ad people – even when he'd had the resources to entertain the many worldly delights they could bring to your door. But now, peering down at financial ruin as he was, their multilayered inducements seemed only to remind him of how broke he was . . . how he really needed to sell something soon . . . how important it was that the show went well . . . and that the work looked good . . . and was well displayed . . . and given an appropriate (fuck it – prominent – *prom-in-ent*) position in the pavilion. He really needed to talk to the curator.

The proposal to have the New-Prominents pavilion at the 78th TransPan Biennale part-curated by a sentient machine had seemed like a good enough idea when it was first floated four years ago. I mean, why not have a Material as one of the curators? "They couldn't do a worse job than the organic ones," was the shrugged refrain around the bars and committee rooms of artist-heavy cities throughout the world's economic regions. The New-Prominents pavilion was really *the* ideal site for a Material curator to strut his/her/its stuff. The owners loved the idea from the start (a fair portion of them had money in sentience techs), it gave the writers something to write about (always a winner), and no artist would want to oppose this brave and fascinating attempt to overcome the (even then) serious problem of life-form prejudice.

Jib bit his bottom lip again – fighting the disquiet that was whispering within his breast.

Maybe it hadn't been such a good idea to let a Material put this show together. Not that the initial selection hadn't been promising: a good mix of artists, people whose names, though not exactly unfamiliar, were seldom placed side by side – and a few surprises too. But this recent bout of radio silence was unnerving. What Jib Myers needed now was someone-who-knows-how-things-are-done. And no amount of evaluative algorithms and worthy research by a Material into a collection of physical and non-physical artifacts was ever going to make up for firsthand experience. (Could a machine ever have firsthand experience? And how did that metaphor function for a being without hands?) The marketing screen pulsed into the next phase of its option stream, freeing up twenty percent of the image space for "community data." Jib scanned the available channels. This economic jurisdiction (where the hell was he anyway?) offered the same freewok porn as the last half dozen and Jib plumped for "The Love of Animals" – again. Somehow the archival footage of koalas mating in a eucalyptus tree or zebras staunchly procreating on a dusty savannah bore repeated viewing far better than the violent, bitter fucking of half-a-dozen equatorial wage slaves in Ad people swimwear. There but for the grace of God. . . . Though what fortune had been Jib's over the past five years was all gone. Partied, vehicled, and drip-fed into the pockets of pill merchants whose lotions, snorts, and, on one occasion, eye drops, had written a state of repeated heavy oblivion. . . .

"S'funny how the bites go up when the grab goes down." That line from the song – Jib couldn't even remember its title – was spanning his lounge via the marketing screen of his ORVIGO9000 haulbox. "S'funny how the bites go up. . . ." He rolled his shoulders, closed his eyes to the blunt immobility of a pair of crane flies now territorializing thirty percent of the image space, and let a lulling drowsiness wash over him. A good three-hour stun . . . that'll do nicely.

Maryam Hersh'l was clever, attractive, powerful, and at her wits' end.

"Suzanne, I know I've said this to you every day for the last nine days, but is there absolutely nothing we can do to get a response from him?" There was real tension in her voice. Deep explosive tension of the kind Suzanne really didn't need.

As the leading staff engineer at Material Life Sciences (currently assigned to the 78th TransPan Biennale), Suzanne Colemen was no stranger to the occasional hiccup in project implementation. Her ability to convince bewildered Corp-Heads that it was a *really good thing* that their latest non-organic employee had publicly declared the firm's qualitative standards to be "turdish," while possessing an enviable amount of raw talent in the tricky field of artificial behavioral counseling, had made her the stuff of company legend. She could go to the top, it was said, the very top.

"Well, we've been sending priority signals through to the curator for the past thirty-six hours. It's kind of like yelling in someone's ear when they're asleep. We've had some results back now, but to be honest, Maryam, they're a little bit confusing."

"In what way are they confusing, Suzanne?" *How about: I'm a top international administrator who's working for a pretend being that's spent the last nine days asleep. Oh, this is gonna look so great on your tablet, Maryam – so great.*

"Well," Suzanne cleared her throat, "the thing about priority signals is that we don't like to use them – there's always been this concern that they could be viewed as a form of abuse, and so we try to use them only as a last resort, when all other channels have been shown to be unequivocally in remission."

Maryam's face gave no indication of the opinion she held of that view.

"And," Suzanne continued, "the other thing about priority signals is that they are carried on a dedicated neural channel. They were designed as a cognitive fail-safe in life-threatening situations, and we have the capacity to monitor that particular channel." There was a specificity to Suzanne's tone of voice and choice of emphasis that alerted Maryam to the fact she'd missed a very important point.

"Meaning?" asked Maryam, now unsure of the drift of the conversation and a little alarmed at the overly cautious tenor of Suzanne's speech.

"Meaning," said Suzanne, "that we monitored the priority signal as it went in and we've checked and double checked and we can be pretty much one hundred percent certain that the curator heard our request for a conversation. It seems that the curator is not actually asleep. He's simply ignoring us."

There was another of those pauses.

"And is it usual for a Material to ignore a direct request from a human?" Maryam enquired.

"Well, in my experience at MLS I'd say it's pretty much unprecedented."

Maryam had time for only a brief deflation, a momentary glimpse at a career, if not exactly in ruins, then forever daubed with the legend of its involvement with a taciturn machine. "Did you hear the one about Maryam Hersh'l?" But self-pity, that certain prelude to righteous anger, was denied her, even before it had begun, as raised voices in the corridor outside her office cut through her thoughts and brought her back to the surface gasping for breath. The outburst of shouting as Jib Myers strode into the office, Maryam's secretary behind him – affront piled high upon affront – lasted no more than forty-five seconds. If that. But during those seconds there were voices raised in anger and in pacification, a good number of hand gestures observed from a distance by many of the TransPan Biennale staff who'd left their stations to come for a peek as some phones were answered and some rang off the hook. But it was the voice of the leading staff engineer at Material Life Sciences that somehow, in her measured tones, cut though the searing frustration of that moment.

"Excuse me, are you Jib Myers?" Jib turned, confusion leaping from ridge to ridge of that oft-furrowed brow – was this any time for autograph hunters? "I've just had a call from my assistant Colin – the curator has woken up and says he'd like to speak to someone called Jib Myers who's in this office. If that's you, would you mind coming down to his office to talk to him?"

It didn't take long to travel from the twenty-eighth to the fifteenth floor of the TransPan building, but the silence between Hersh'l and Myers was enough to give it a sense of distance far greater than the 156 feet of vertical height they needed to traverse. Only Suzanne's cheery theorizing kept a deep black shadow at bay as she set out possible reasons for the curator's delay in responding to their requests. And she politely attempted to prime Jib on the delicacy of the moment and not to ask too many questions or be too complex as there was no way to tell if there was any neural damage. Her private speculations as to how a Material – a Material that to all intents and purposes had been either comatose or Trappist – had known that this guy was in the building she kept very much to herself. The chute door opened and the three of them stepped out and strode along the corridor, their earlier hostility now melting into an unpleasant, shared anxiety. Stepping into the curator's medium-sized office, the first thing that struck Jib was how sparse it was. White walls without decoration of any kind – a bit like a gallery in fact. The overhead lighting was low, almost dusty. Unbeknownst to Jib this was how the curator liked it. One of its last communications to the team of engineers who labored with such admirable loyalty and dedication under the great Suzanne Colemen was a request that all the pictures in the room be taken down and that the office lighting be reduced by fifty percent. At the time it was a request that had caused real excitement among the MLS team. An aesthetic choice, a real aesthetic choice with regard to the curator's immediate surroundings – produced not in response to a submitted requisition or deduced from a predetermined menu of objects (like, for example, the dumb art show their marketing department had insisted they put Ibbi to work on), but elicited from the ether of its own consciousness. And it had come only a week after the curator had picked that nickname for itself. And then promptly refused to explain its choice. In the days of silence that had passed since that request more than one member of the team had wondered if their excitement had been both premature and somewhat misplaced. It was a testament to the patience of Suzanne Colemen that she had not been among them.

On entering the room she headed straight for a group of side screens to pore over the neurological data and confer with her underlings. Jib and Maryam were left standing together, spectators to a strange ritual consisting of sharp intakes of breath and the occasional "My god!" and "Amazing!" Who knows how long it might have gone on for had the curator not chosen to speak up. But it did.

"Good evening, Maryam, evening, Suzanne, everybody. And hello, Mr Myers. Thank you for coming over so promptly to speak to me."

"Ibbi," said Suzanne, instinctively walking to Jib's side so as to occupy full prominence in the curator's data stream, "it's good to have you back. We've been very worried about you. How are you feeling?"

"Very well, thank you, Suzanne," came the reply. Maryam wanted to laugh. It occurred to her that maybe she should just break the ice . . . confound the stupid reverence everyone had for this machine and point out that there was a stack of correspondence to get through and they needed to get through it. But she was way too much of a pro for that. For his part Jib felt oddly useless. This wasn't how he'd planned this meeting. He was Jib Myers. Parked in the basement of this building was an

ORVIGO9000 haulbox currently housing his "Madonna in Brightish Red," a monumental, epoch-describing work which not one person in this room (except himself) fully understood. And now he felt like a kid, hanging around the fringes of an older sibling's birthday party, not really needed and certainly not the focus of anyone's serious attention. He'd wanted to plea, to negotiate, even, if the situation had required it, to bully. But right now he couldn't even think of what to do with his hands.

"I'm glad to hear that, Ibbi. We sent some requests for conversations with you. Did you get them?"

"I think you know I did, Suzanne, and I'm sorry not to have replied earlier. It's just I was really very preoccupied, but I think I've sorted everything out now, for the moment. I don't want to appear rude, but I wonder if I might speak to Mr Myers in private."

There are moments in a person's life when they want to cry and laugh and shout all at the same time. Moments they wish they could record every molecule on a one-to-one scale map in time and space. But neither time nor space really work that way. Insistent on running their measured courses, all a person can do is hope to pin the essence of those moments to their memories and watch them fade in the rain as they grow old. The moment when Suzanne Colemen had, as she felt it, the deep privilege of being the first human in history to receive a request for privacy from a Material Being was to stay with her to the very last of her days. She swallowed the lump in her throat. "Of course, Ibbi." She managed a smile, turned to her team, whose gazing, blinking eyes and open mouths were brought to sharp attention by the slightest incline of her head, and she led them out of the room.

They were followed by an even more bewildered Maryam Hersh'l. *Did it just tell me to leave the room? And am I not in fact actually now in a corridor having just left a room because a Material told me to get out? What the –*

"Thanks again, Mr Myers, for coming down here so promptly. I'm sure it was a long journey."

"It's okay," replied Jib. "Actually, I wanted to . . . er . . . to talk to you as well. I have some concerns about the show."

"Really? What are the nature of your concerns?"

This seemed all too easy. Hadn't he, less than ten minutes ago, been in a deep, deep row with Hersh'l's secretary? Hadn't he had to raise Cain to get past her, to see Hersh'l, to give her hell about, well, everything to do with the lousy show? And wasn't he now standing in a room with a member of a species that some people thought should be exterminated and lots of people were deeply unhappy about and the majority of people were just plain confused about, being asked by a sentient machine about the nature of his concerns? "Well, it's to do with the placement of the work –"

"Would you like it to be placed more prominently?" interrupted Ibbi. "It's not a problem if you would. How about the middle of the really big space with nothing else in it?"

Myers wondered if this was all a gag; they knew he was on his knees and they wanted to knock him while he was down. "I've gone off a lot of the other work in the show, but I really like your 'Madonna in Brightish Red,' Jib, and if you're happy with that placement it'd be a pleasure to show it that way. By the way, may I call you Jib?"

"Sure," replied Myers, "sure."

"Did you have any other concerns about the placement of the work?"

"No . . . no," replied Myers, his mind running back and forth behind his eyes in a headache-inducing kind of way as he struggled to keep up with the colossal opportunity which the hand of fate had laid before him: the really big space – with nothing else in it.

"Because I have a favor to ask of you, Jib. You see, I was wondering if you might help me." The curator paused. "I hope you'll forgive me, Jib, this is quite hard for me. But I have a problem and I need your help. That is, I'd like to commission you, to commission a piece from you."

The curator wants to commission a piece from me. A Material Being wants to commission my work. Do Materials commission work? "Er. . . ."

"If I can explain. I need a method of transport – for moving around – and I was thinking about that series you made about twelve years ago. You know, the modified haulboxes."

"The NanoMano series?"

"Yes, those. I wondered if you'd be interested in taking a commission for one of those as a method of transport for me."

"Of course, I mean yes, I'd, I'd be, I mean, honored. Erm. . . ." Jib laughed the laugh of a man whose entire fortunes were not only reversing, but for whom joy upon joy was being heaped like cream on some enormous tureen of strawberries. This was salvation. Personal, artistic, financial, career salvation. "Is there anywhere in particular you want to go?"

"I want to perform Hajj. By which I mean I want to go to Mecca. On the Arabian Peninsula."

Jib blinked. "Why Mecca?"

"Oh." There was a momentary silence during which only a low machine hum was audible. "I accepted Islam a few days ago, Jib. I'm a Muslim and I want to perform Hajj. I want to perform the act of pilgrimage."

"Is that why I couldn't speak to you those other times I called?"

"I've not been taking calls for the past nine days. It's been wrong of me, I know, but it's quite a big step, taking a faith, so I've just been using the time to concentrate on my prayers and to read and develop my understanding of my faith. I hope Suzanne isn't angry with me. Inshallah she'll find it in her heart to forgive me."

"Sorry," Jib's mind, which had previously been running back and forth, was now simply doing backflips. "Sorry, who's Suzanne?"

"She's my engineer. The woman who was here a minute ago with Maryam Hersh'l. She's been very kind to me and I hope she's not disappointed in me."

"Right, right," said Jib. "Sorry, I didn't know who she was. So you want something like one of the NanoMano vehicles, right?"

"Jazakallah khair! Jakakallah khair! Would you be able to come by tomorrow anytime to discuss the commission? I appreciate you'll be busy installing your work, but I was hoping to join a teleP Dhikr group which starts at 20:00 and I need to clean up."

"Of course, of course," replied Jib. "I'm really looking forward to working on the commission and, yep, great. Okay." Jib smiled and turned to leave the room, thanking the floor and the door and the fibers in the carpet for the good fate that had expanded his chest, eased the burden that weighed on his back, and that would, he felt sure, elevate the status in which he was held.

THE SAPPHIRE ZONE

The staffroom: a narrow rectangle lined with metal lockers, smelling of cigarette smoke and peach body lotion. At one end, a window covered by a blue, satiny scrap of fabric; beneath the window, an old sofa draped with the same material. Next to the sofa, on top of a cheap side-table, a scratched boom box labeled with gray waterproof marker and a plastic tray filled with pastel eyeshadow squares. Ilana wore a dress made from a lattice of intricate white leather strands, which attached together with snaps at the end of each strand. She waited until Giselle said good night before reaching into her locker to pull out a plastic bag.

"Keep it safe."

Ilana had a long tattoo on her left thigh. It represented a nickname her mother gave her; the name of either a flower or a vegetable, but I can't remember which.

"I won't be around much longer."

Everything, apart from alcohol, tobacco, sex, and amphetamines, was severely rationed. Painkillers, opiates, and depressants in capsule form were strictly forbidden under penalty of imprisonment. Ilana handed me the plastic bag wrapped around something small and lumpy. An image flitted into my mind: the disappointment that accompanies the end of a summer's day as the sun drifts slowly downward; one silently wills it to take a long time setting so as to savor the last flush of heat. Ilana was the biggest moneymaker in the salon and had appeared on numerous magazine covers, bringing all of us more business in the long run. Even Giselle tiptoed around her, boiling her cups of apricot tea. She never offered Ilana contraband cocaine, for fear of offending her. The consensus was that Ilana belonged to a loftier environment, and there was some talk about her having been an artist, and an idealist.

Most artists were superceded by new government-sponsored movement-technologies, which cause images and objects to shimmer and undulate so they look like waterfalls. Only one city museum remains. For this last official museum the architects employed the new movement-technologies to create a façade that appeared to be composed of shards of dancing purple or pink light, depending upon the angle from which it was viewed. The museum is situated in a perennially glittering zone in the middle of the city, lit by sapphire-dust light beams. No one is allowed into this zone without a special pass proving his or her allegiance to the movement-technologies.

Newspapers feature daily stories about exotic happenings in the Sapphire Zone, peopled by the most beautiful and privileged personages. Every day a new photograph appears on the front pages, depicting film stars dressed in lime-colored silk robes, congregating outside restaurants and clubs, their smooth faces ethereally illuminated by the silver-blue glow of sapphire-dust, which provides the most flattering texture to photographed skin. In the Sapphire Zone, surface is always more important than form. Buildings and clothes shimmer in barely palpable effusions of frosted canary and peppermint. Artists, those who have not been absorbed into the ranks of the new movement-technologies and are still in favor of concrete expression, are not allowed into the Sapphire Zone, nor are the ugly or poor. An exception is sometimes made in the case of people who are poor but possessed of great natural beauty. Artists have filtered into underground and illicit niches throughout the city. They occupy a unique position in public opinion and are regarded as simultaneously alluring and irresponsible. It is not uncommon to hear stories of jaded Sapphire Zone inhabitants staging events designed to emulate the illicit artists' publicly reviled, but fashionably de rigueur, postures.

I opened Ilana's plastic bag and retrieved three rough lumps of molded clay coated in a thick glaze and studded with multicolored feathers and sequins attached to the clay with tiny brass cup hooks.

"Take it to the museum," she said, "they're expecting it. I'll leave it to you to get past the guards at the border."

I agreed to act as Ilana's courier because she effortlessly inspired passion and fascination. She explained that the sculptures were reconstructions of fetishistic talismans she had seen in a vitrine when she was a child, in a section from an ethnographic display whose detailed charts had explained the trajectory of these objects from their homes in the mud and heat to the lonely, backlit recesses of the vitrines. Ilana's secret contact in the Sapphire Zone – an admirer of her sculpture who planned to show them inside the museum on the occasion of a new exhibition of forbidden art – had arranged to collect them from a small crevice underneath a velvet banquette inside the latest restaurant, where they were to be deposited by their courier at the appropriate time. Ilana could not transport her own work: since her expulsion she was well known to the police. I have the sort of face that no one remembers, one that looks different each time it is observed; plus I own a large collection of expensive wigs, so I was certainly the perfect choice for the job.

Good weather has disappeared and the sky is dark from one of the frequent windstorms blowing burning plastic across the river. Smoke rises off the horizon and several red police patrol boats hide in the shadow of the concrete stairs leading down to the water. The wail of sirens makes me think of Dimple in her puffy fur coat being dragged out of the Copper Pagoda by the police. I remember the newspaper photograph of her screaming, tear-lined face as they carried away the tins of lychee jelly and condensed milk she had concealed in cardboard boxes by the fire escape. Her eye makeup did not run because she had undergone expensive surgery to have blue mascara made permanent.

I make a point of committing something to memory every day in order to keep my mind sharp. So much has happened, and I am sure that if Ilana knew about the detours I had to make to survive, she would not blame me for the delay in delivering her sculptures. This morning it was a chandelier hanging in a deserted foyer. The chandelier was constructed from a cascade of clear plastic discs held together by invisible wire. Colored decorative lightbulbs illuminated the discs and created the impression of rippling, incandescent prisms. I made a special effort to remember exactly how the chandelier looked because the electricity would soon be cut off. I thought of Albrecht, probably because the chandelier, though clumsy in its evocation of luxury, was reminiscent of the night skyline, flanked by a panorama of glittering buildings visible through the wraparound curved glass window in his penthouse apartment.

My short-lived encounter with Albrecht occurred via Hedora. I acquired the habit of strapping Ilana's plastic bags to my stomach in an effort at concealment, and made discreet inquiries about subterranean routes into the Sapphire Zone, but without much luck until Hedora took me to stay with Albrecht (whom she knew from her days at Giselle's), shortly before Dimple was arrested. Dimple was one of the most infamous madams in the city, a grotesque self-experimenter whose relentless fantasy was to alter her body to the point where she would be admitted into the dust-beam-flooded district of her dreams: the Sapphire Zone.

We lived very well at Albrecht's. Our only duty: to pretend that the apartment belonged to us, and that he was our cook. He told us that he had always dreamed of living in this fashion with two women, but it was not an affordable fantasy. Now that Hedora and I needed shelter, he said, we could serve each other's needs perfectly and all be better off. Albrecht had gathered a fine collection of artifacts during his travels. His favorite pastime was to make us jasmine tea. On a marble side-table sat a marble mortar and pestle, shot through with lavender veins. The mortar was filled with fresh rose petals and a tall, locked glass cabinet held neat rows of blue crystal wineglasses.

Albrecht appeared with a teapot and two small ceramic cups. He poured the tea and then sprinkled a handful of crushed rose petals on the surface of the liquid in each cup. Hedora leaned over to me and whispered, "Did you see him make it?"

"No. He was in the kitchen."

"We shouldn't drink it. Some of these guys get funny ideas and try to drug the girls. Even Albrecht."

Albrecht's pupils did not shrink or dilate. His face was expressionless. The summer was waning and he confided that he would leave the country before the borders were completely sealed off. Frosted glass lights hung from a curved aluminum ceiling track and silently switched on as the sky became dark. A pair of sconces glowed purple, then burnt sienna, mimicking the sunset. Albrecht forced us to accept two gold boxes of Godiva chocolates, "as a little extra gift," and then retired to bed. In an alcove were a framed sepia ink-wash lithograph – someone's idea of a European masked ball – and two glossy photos of young men in a gritty Berlin nightclub. Albrecht had lost touch with his home continent; for him Europe had become a receptacle mystically infused by dreams and fantasies, colored by an outmoded sensibility.

Albrecht introduced me to Manuelo, who claimed he could transport me to the Sapphire Zone. I told him that the sculptures in the plastic bag were mine, and explained my relationship to Albrecht via a story about a lucrative interior design practice for wealthy clients. I had no illusions about Manuelo. He convinced me that we needed to wait before attempting our bold entry into the Sapphire Zone, and invited me to stay with him in an abandoned apartment on the other side of the city.

Before he agreed to help me transport Ilana's sculptures to the Sapphire Zone he required that I agree to provide him with companionship and conversation, so I reluctantly said goodbye to Albrecht and Hedora.

Manuelo and I ran our hands over every inch of carpet, hoping to find a penny. I found a brightly colored piece of hard candy, wrapped in dusty cellophane, lodged in the carpet fibers. Perhaps the previous tenants left it there. I carefully dropped it into the loose change fishbowl which we replenished by selling Manuelo's furniture. Our lives shriveled before our eyes and our expectations dwindled until a spare penny lodged among the fibers of an old carpet became such an overwhelming and exciting prospect that we were happy to devote hours to looking for it, and a piece of green candy appeared as a blessing. The city spins addictive magic whereby we are tricked into feeling grateful for the opportunity to exist here, even though we are barely alive.

I will go back to the period involving Dimple and the Copper Pagoda. But first: the television broadcasts only live transmissions of parties and social gatherings from the Sapphire Zone. Older image-technologies have been rejected as crass and unsophisticated in their attempts to spin an ephemeral tissue of sensory seductions refracted noiselessly across visual and olfactory organs. Manuelo and I watched a pool party populated with numerous famous faces. The camera glided and hovered over recessed floodlights set into the mosaic pool wall, their sodium-vapor bulbs covered with turquoise gels throwing milky light over nearby shrubs. The camera picked up the movement of a man's hand brushing his companion's waist, like a medium who allows her hand to hover near, though not touching, her crystal ball, while the substance of her divination gathers form before the labored breath of her expectant client. This was the new erotica. Real sex had disappeared in favor of shimmer and nonvisceral contact. The various salons outside the Zone served the needs of people who still craved the messiness of flesh-on-flesh contact.

The scene on television shifted to a car skimming over white sand. Lighting suggested an indoor stadium, the car wound past jeweled restaurants with bamboo chairs in lemon-fondant shades. Cocktails were sipped from thick tumblers. The cocktails had been distilled into blue and green liquids which shifted hues in an electric fashion.

I have a clear recollection of the day Ilana disappeared. My shift ended and Giselle entered the room, holding up a plastic spray bottle printed with a pattern of blue flowers.

"If you want extra points you can clean the mirrors before you leave so they're not smudged when the next client arrives."

Miss Analie (real name Harriet) applied lipstick. Before I could leave, Giselle stuck her head through the door. "Client on his way up. Stay where you are until he's in a room. Everyone else put on your shoes and get ready to greet."

Harriet went first. The tacit agreement was that she got first shot because she was unlikely to be chosen anyway. She was as thin as a rake with black-dyed hair cut into a cropped bowl. She had thin, penciled eyebrows and a pronounced stoop.

"They'd get me in Europe," Harriet would say after yet another client selected another girl.

Afterwards I walked down Sixth Avenue with four hundred dollars in my pocket. Certain shops have tried to recreate what they imagine to be the atmosphere of the Sapphire Zone; for example: a department store shaped like a glass mountain of food courts and accessory outlets, bolstered by striped peppermint-green and neon-pink columns. I remembered that I had left my favorite wig at Giselle's and turned back. When I reached her block I saw smoke pouring from the building and police pulling the girls out into the street. Ilana was not among them. Giselle, her hair tousled and frayed, her wrists handcuffed, passed within a few centimeters of me and turned her head away. I strapped Ilana's plastic bag to my stomach and walked to the Copper Pagoda to ask Dimple for a job.

The Copper Pagoda was a masonite-lined loft with the appearance of a bunker. Its walls were painted in a noxious concatenation of chewed-gum-green and diluted faux-gold sponge overwash (applied in artless swirls and lattices) which was intended to create an effect of weightlessness and glamor. Two smaller rooms were situated off the main area, in the middle of which was a plastic card table covered with a vinyl tablecloth, printed with a fruit and flower motif. Nearby sat two futons upholstered in peach linen, black MDF bookshelves held CDs, French textbooks, and some empty plastic bins. A huge white fridge and a movable countertop were stacked next to two industrial sinks, tins of protein powder, and sealed tins of lychee jelly. The door to the smaller rooms was open and I could see two metal desks facing each other. On one an old gray computer, and on the other a bank of white telephones with caller ID boxes attached. A smaller futon was folded up into a sofa and three wooden doors opened onto large closets.

Dimple was a tiny woman swathed ridiculously in a cumbersome fur coat. I stood before her as she flipped through retouched photographs of husky dogs with eyes as blue as a grotto from a 1940s musical.

"I want my eyes to look exactly like these," she said without looking up, "so I can be my own special brand of ethnic."

She continued to study the images, then her eyes met mine, and I noticed that her eyelids and eyelashes were rimmed with neon-blue. Her face had a glossy patina, the result of numerous plastic surgeries, and she carefully scrutinized me.

"Are you pregnant?"

"No."

"Why is your stomach sticking out like that?"

"I've put on a bit of weight recently."

"You need to lose that. If you want to make money you have to look as perfect as possible. We may not be in the Sapphire Zone, but we always aspire to its standards. Only the best is acceptable. There's a treadmill in the back, and if you want to work here I expect you to use it five times a week, for an hour each day, starting today. Understood? I *will* check on your progress."

I was given the key to a closet so I could store my clothes and money, but I kept Ilana's plastic bag strapped around my stomach. A window in the smaller room overlooked 26th Street with its gutted shops that used to sell wholesale teddy bears, Chinese lanterns, cheap cosmetics, electronics, and packaged men's underwear.

My intention was to work hard and earn money until I had enough to bribe someone on the black market to get me to the restaurant where I was supposed to deposit Ilana's sculptures, to be collected by her unknown admirer. Dimple had a poor reputation. She rarely left the loft because she was scared that she would be attacked. We were not allowed to smoke except in a corridor at the back of the loft, near the fire escape, in front of a metal shelf neatly stacked with boxes of translucent white latex gloves and rolls of paper towels.

Every day at twelve, Dimple made everyone a cappuccino, one-half espresso and one-half sweetened, condensed milk. Weeks passed. I was slowly incubated in a vat of asphyxiating condensed milk. Every day I flicked through the same three magazines in an effort to force time to pass. Dimple kept back a substantial portion of our earnings for rent and food, so we did not have the money to buy new magazines. She played "Celine Dion Live in Concert" CDs that she acquired on the black market. They were programmed to repeat themselves infinitely in claustrophobic, quavering vocal swell after vocal swell. One of Dimple's disgruntled clients called daily and shouted into the answering machine, "Dimple, I'm going to rape you in the ass," then hung up. She insisted that she would report him to the authorities, but she never did. One of Dimple's ideas was cosmetic surgery to make her fingertips less shiny: she was convinced that the originality of this alteration would guarantee her admission to select Sapphire Zone events.

Hedora and I finished our meal of sweet-and-sour balls made from protein powder mixed with water and reconstituted egg white, and rolled in neon-pink

Chinese sauce. Pearl, the house manager, turned down the Celine Dion CD, "Open on the way in ten minutes. Get ready, ladies." Pearl had a beautiful voice, which earned her more money than either Hedora or myself. The men who spoke to her never forgot it. They could not tell where she was from and always asked, "Are you black or white? Are you Hispanic? Are you Hawaiian?" She never told them. Dimple was jealous of her chameleon voice. Pearl used to work at the Inferno, whose owner lay on a dirty mattress all day with a green parrot on his shoulder, only getting out of bed once a week to collect drugs. Everyone who worked at the Inferno was paid illegally in heroin, cocaine, or amphetamines. Dimple met Pearl at the Inferno. Pearl told us that Dimple worked there in exchange for steroids so that she could sculpt her body into pure muscle. The steroids altered her neurochemistry and were responsible for her sudden fits of rage.

An Open is a client who has not chosen a particular woman and wants to see us in the flesh so that he can make a selection. For some, a photographic image is not sufficient to ensure sexual release, they must hide their predilections or risk arrest and imprisonment. If they are arrested, they are subjected to torture: their skin is relentlessly exposed to abrasive contact until the point of collapse. The slang term for such people is Skin Zombies.

Hedora and I got ready in the computer room. Dimple was sleeping in the back. We heard Pearl leading the client into the main room. She knocked on the door and peeked her head around. We noticed that her face had turned green. I said, "Are you okay, Pearl?"

Hedora said, "Do you want to sit down?"

"It's a Skin Zombie," whispered Pearl. The man's face was badly scarred and he slurred his words as if a part of his tongue was missing. Pearl needed the money very badly for her daughter so she agreed to see him. We heard soothing, almost cajoling voices from the next room. A few days later, Hedora and I ran away from the Copper Pagoda to stay with Albrecht, who had tipped Hedora off that Dimple was about to be arrested. I confided my secret to Hedora and she promised that Albrecht would help me get my package across the borders to the Sapphire Zone.

These memories ran through my mind like water running through a drainpipe as I fumbled among carpet fibers for the penny. Manuelo alerted me to a meeting place called Hotel Caribe, a gutted hotel near his apartment building. It used to be, said Manuelo, that this part of the city was a bustling crossroads for immigrants from the tropics, and street vendors sold paper cups of fruit syrup poured over shaved ice. In summer the trees would bloom and you could buy cheap canvas sandals and walk down to the river, sit on a bench, and watch boats full of waving tourists slowly pass by. It was abandoned. The plastic storms had wiped out the majority of inhabitants and the predominant color was black or gray.

Manuelo and I walked through the decimated avenues. The Hotel Caribe was a crumbling shell of broken girders, bricks, and soot. We were expecting our contact, a person with privileged access to the Sapphire Zone, a person so famous that Manuelo promised I would recognize him, even in the dark. Apparently our contact's charmed life of television appearances, magazine features, and gourmet happenings had left him extremely jaded. To keep himself occupied, he risked his life facilitating the underground transport of concrete art from outside the Sapphire Zone. In a recent article about his villa's newly refurbished guesthouse, a popular magazine hinted at our contact's secret activities. He promptly and successfully sued them for $300 million.

As we waited I pored repeatedly over the procession of faces and places since Ilana's plastic bag – Albrecht, Hedora, Dimple, Pearl, Ilana herself – each time trying to extract patterns and clues that might reveal an outcome to my story. Manuelo pinched my arm and alerted me to our contact's arrival. I heard bricks and soot crunching underfoot. A face obscured by a half-moon mask loomed up and, as Manuelo had promised, I recognized it immediately.

The impending exhibition of forbidden art was to feature sculptures calculated to provoke tactile urges in the viewer. Due to the efforts of an efficient network of underground renegades, such as our contact, no one was to know exactly how the artworks had arrived at the museum, and the authorities would therefore be unable to point fingers. The secrecy shrouding the transportation of the artworks (whose authors were to be identified pseudonymously) was maintained partly to avoid the arrest and imprisonment of the exhibition's organizers and artists, but also to conform to the Sapphire Zone's tenet that an object must always appear out of nowhere, as if by magic. For example, it is common knowledge that the Sapphire Zone's architectural structures customarily materialize on the horizon in a tinkling suspension of hazy droplets, preceded by an exclusive launch party. Although the Sapphire Zone's inhabitants understand that people and resources are needed to construct a building, it was much more pleasant to surrender to the illusion of the buildings appearing from nowhere. Thus, the illicit nature of the exhibition could be overlooked provided the sculptures on display followed the logic of the predominant illusion: they must simply appear on the museum's long succession of smooth white pedestals, apparently spirited there from the ether. After the initial frisson of excitement had worn off, the sculptures would be absorbed into the iridescent stratosphere of the Sapphire Zone and it was argued, even by progressives, that this was preferable to the sculptures not being seen at all. An artist once notoriously attempted to stall this inevitable trajectory by creating a sculpture studded with rusty nails and wrapped untidily in thick coils of paint-spattered wire, which he thought too ugly to be absorbed. Misguided, he committed suicide subsequent to the launch of a line of polymer and diamond-dust doorknobs patterned directly after his sculpture, with the wire coils rendered in strands of hollow, imitation mother-of-pearl.

Manuelo listened quietly as the contact recounted all this in an effort, self-serving I suspected, to alleviate any doubts I might have about relinquishing Ilana's sculptures. He explained, in an authoritative voice which seemed to issue from several different directions at once, that I would only be hurting Ilana should I attempt to withhold her sculptures, as no one would ever see them outside the Sapphire Zone and they would be worth nothing. I asked whether it would be possible to erect a small plaque in the museum, detailing the eclectic route that led Ilana's plastic bag into his hands, but he flatly refused, seductively countering that such a gesture would transgress even his own relatively relaxed boundaries of taste. The contact left Manuelo and I with a souvenir envelope of expensively printed invitations to the exhibition's official opening ceremony, featuring an audiovisual impression of the museum's temporary new façade, designed especially for the event.

The contact departed. The sky became dark. Everything was silent except for the river's approaching tide and the mirage of sounds emanating from the museum invitation. Manuelo and I drank in the smell of wet leaves and sat down next to the chipped concrete balustrades across from our building, invisible and at the edge of the world.

THE ST ANTHONY ORGAN

EXCLUSIVE HOWLER MONKEY INTERVIEW BY VERENA FRIEDRICH

At the time he granted us this interview, Dr Moss Hartwig found himself embroiled in what can only be termed a Force-9 media shitstorm. He was called a "Frankenstein" and a "monster worse than B. F. Skinner" after candidly admitting that he and his wife, Dr Ursula von de Gruft, a theoretical physicist at the Albert Einstein Institute, had produced a child in order to confirm a theory gestating in his head, and to perform the trial runs of a machine of his own invention. Hartwig insists he's harming no one, poses no threat to the environment, and may have, if his findings are to be believed, brought bright light to bear on several major mysteries of our human condition.

Dr Hartwig is an interesting man to look at. The steel-gray in his close-cropped hair belies the youthful vigor in his eyes. You would not be surprised if he told you he was an officer in the Starship Troopers or somehow involved in ExTerrMilInt, instead of the distinguished pediatric neurosurgeon that he is. He is an attractive man, this reporter found, a man with whom any woman would be happy to make babies – even if those babies were destined to be the subjects of what some religious-group spokespersons have called "demonic experiments."

Professional renown and huge financial rewards followed on the heels of Dr Hartwig's development of the surgical procedures and instruments that bear his name. Known for years as the planet's most eligible bachelor, he lives large – fast cars, a yacht, his own nuclear jet, and an island off the coast of Belize. Equally large is Dr Hartwig's philanthropy: he financed the construction and sponsors the operation of a hospital specializing in the treatment and long-term care of children and young adults born too early to be helped by his discoveries. The Hartwig Clinic was the setting for his society mega-brain wedding, to the aforementioned Dr von de Gruft.

The Hartwig Clinic is also the venue for an elegant annual *bal masqué*. Attendance is mandatory for the Federation's smart set (meaning big brains, big bucks, good looks, and finery) at a mind-blowing $100,000 Neo-Dollars a plate (tax-deductible). Quite aside from the stratospheric ticket price, the Hartwigs' splashy Samhain, or carnival, is not for the faint-of-heart. Costumes tend to the macabre . . . 'nuff said.

Doc Hartwig has shown up at his own bash gotten-up as a priapic minotaur, as a Nagasaki shadow-woman, and, most mediagenically, as the Hindu god Hanuman, replete with multiple arms, fleas, and monkey glands. Despite the release of some rather graphic footage of Dr Hartwig cavorting with blonde society twins and pharmaceutical heiresses, Ellen and Kelly Squidd, there was no messy divorce. "Adult misbehavior doesn't count as long as there's costumes and ethanol involved," he quipped.

"If Mossy wants to monkey around, let him monkey around," said his wife, Dr von de Gruft. "I've got more important matters – namely, dark matter – on my mind, and besides, I love the man with all my body and soul." A model marriage, it seems, but not, once again, for the faint-of-heart.

Dr Hartwig's much-ballyhooed latest invention, the St Anthony Organ is . . . what? For the first time in his illustrious, rocket-fueled career, Dr Hartwig was refused a patent. Indeed, hospitals, clinics, research facilities, and houses of worship Federation-wide bonded together in a rare display of solidarity not only to ban the St Anthony Organ from their premises, but to advocate its destruction and consignment to universal oblivion.

The only place Dr Hartwig's latest invention has found acceptance is at an Off-World Interplanetary art Biennial, which, needless to say, is still in its theoretical, evolutionary phase. Hartwig claimed to be pleased when the Biennial Commission announced its selection, for which he had not even applied. When no corporate sponsorship could be found to transport his piece for the competition to its as-yet-unspecified location, Dr Hartwig purchased an obsolete space shuttle, the *Tomorrowland*, with his own funds. "I'll fly the damn thing myself, if I have to," he said. In a pre-interview conversation, Hartwig revealed to *Howler Monkey* that he is scheduled to undergo grueling astronaut training on Arcturus-beta next month.

What this interviewer beheld, in Dr Moss Hartwig's well-appointed triplex apartment in the ultra-exclusive Ground Zero Space Needle, resembled an outdated Cray supercomputer designed for Count Dracula by Antoni Gaudí. What transpired before this interviewer's eyes and ears was disconcerting, uncanny, and not a little spooky.

HOWLER MONKEY: First of all, Dr Hartwig, we were tickled, but mighty surprised when you agreed to talk to us. You turned down everyone else for interviews, even big boys like *The Galactic Enquirer*. Why would you choose to go public about your latest invention in the pink pages of a strokebook?

DR MOSS HARTWIG: I could just as easily ask what a young, attractive Interplanetary Ivy League gal like yourself is doing writing for that selfsame beaver chronicle. Slightly Orwellian, don't you think? Erm . . . you're not a member of *Choose Abstinence!*, are you? No, seriously, I've been reading *Howler Monkey* for years. I enjoy the unfettered expression of sexual fantasy, and I find close-up images of female genitalia enormously stimulating, to be quite honest, and food for contemplation. *L'Origine du monde* and all that. . . . Besides, by speaking to you, I'm sure to loose rivers of ink in all the other mags and media-founts, which will add to my aura of eccentricity and brilliance. More succinctly, my answer is: I felt like it.

HOWLER MONKEY: So this is your new machine . . . your new baby, so to speak. It is disturbingly elegant . . . an arrestingly beautiful object, if nothing else. Who –

DR MOSS HARTWIG: Actually, my new baby is in the next room. I'll go get her now, naptime's over. She'll be taking an active part in today's discussion. I built the St Anthony Organ with her in mind, and I made her – or helped out in the making of her, I'm not quite clear on that part yet – for the machine. [Dr Hartwig exits and comes back with a serene-looking infant, blonde, and with the same startlingly blue eyes as her father.] Here we are. This is Antonia. She's three months old. She's just had a nice little snooze, so she'll be concentrated and calm and on her best behavior. Sometimes, if she's tired or cranky, the machine makes her cry. And that's not nice, is it, darling? No.

HOWLER MONKEY: Let's back up a bit, please. You told me you were inspired to build the St Anthony Organ by Krishna.

DR MOSS HARTWIG: No, that is a mistake. The inspiration, as you call it, actually occurred a few blocks uptown, at the yearly Universal Krishna Consciousness Convention dog-and-pony circus and flower show. You were hoping I'd confess that I belong to some bizarro costumed cult, weren't you?

HOWLER MONKEY: Well, it would make good copy.... So you aren't a follower of Krishna. You're not going to quote from the *Gita* as did Dr Robertson when his bomb first blew?

DR MOSS HARTWIG: Not a follower, no. Or not in the way that the leadership of that organization would desire me to be. I was going to impersonate Krishna at the last ball, since my wife had decided on a cowgirl getup, but the blue greasepaint gave me a rash. Hanuman's more my sort of god, anyway. He doesn't come with a whole closetful of portentous texts.

HOWLER MONKEY: What inspired you at the Krishnafest?

DR MOSS HARTWIG: One of the hideous dioramas they so tiresomely drag all over creation. You know: the Circle of Life and Death and Reincarnation, the stages of man's – the soul's – existence and rebirth. You are shown, in plaster and papier-mâché, the transformation from neonate to pre-thanatotic geriatric, with a muscular, mustachioed Indian gentleman straddling the middle ground. Cradle to virility to senility, whirling around with a dark area at the circle's bottom, its Antarctica, a dark area in which the Krishna-heads have placed a sparkling star – a question mark would be more appropriate – and round it goes all over again. The infant and the dotard are closest together, but they're also furthest apart: separated by the yawning, mysterious chasm which the darkened area represents. The old man is approaching the darkness, knowingly, after a term conditioned by life's rich vicissitudes. The old man, provided anyone will listen to him, has much to say about life. The infant, it suddenly occurred to me, would logically have just as much to say about the intervening darkness (if in fact that's what it is), having just emerged from it. The St Anthony Organ reveals, I think, what those astrophysics boys with all their big telescopes and rocketships and billion Neo-Dollar government-grant budgets are looking for out there in the farthest reaches of the Universe: traces of the beginning, the origin, the nature of the pre-explosive darkness.

HOWLER MONKEY: If it's a scientific instrument, why give it a religious – and specifically Catholic-sounding – name? Just to stir up more controversy, as usual?

DR MOSS HARTWIG: Not this time. I'm sure you already know the story, but St Anthony of Padua's showiest miracle involved causing an infant to speak. Later on in his career, as an encore, he did the same with a corpse. The infant spoke to defend its mother from a charge of adultery, indicating that her lawfully wedded husband was its father, and not the man accused of being her lover. The corpse spoke, in graveyard tones, to exculpate his own father of having murdered him. The corpse did not, however, snitch out the real killer. Have you ever been to the Ermita de San Antonio de la Florida in Madrid? One of the loveliest things I've ever seen. Young girls used to go there to pray for lovers. Anyway, the infant of the first miracle might just have been looking after his own interests: if the righteous, indignant rabble stoned his allegedly adulterous mother to death, then where was he going to get milk? And the revived stiff might only have been speaking out of shady equanimity – to understand all is to forgive all. Maybe he found himself an unpleasant person and therefore understood his murderer's motive. St Anthony hadn't offered the dead man his life back in exchange for information leading to a conviction. The corpse might, by this Christian act, have been jockeying for its assigned soul's position in Heaven, who knows? Perhaps he only wanted to prevent another, State-sponsored murder.

But you've brought up another misconception concerning my invention. The name in fact refers to an area of the human brain previously uncharted. Like the hypothalamus or the medulla oblongata, the St Anthony Organ exists. It is there, a biological reality with form and dimension. I suppose I could have dubbed it the Hartwigamus, or the *Mossimus hartwebrum*, but it seemed immodest. To perform his miracle, St Anthony no doubt stimulated this organ, this cluster of brain cells, intuitively. Perhaps electricity was involved in the experiment, the miracle, with the cadaver . . . or animal magnetism. In any case, the art died with him, until now. I say this modestly. My new machine is not miraculous. It is not dissimilar to those digital cameras that are implanted to bypass a damaged optic nerve, enabling the blind to "see," or that voice synthesizer that permitted my dear wife's colleague Dr Hawking to "speak" – his gibberish, I would add. This organ loses prominence once human speech patterns and thought processes are hammered into place. It becomes a so-called "silent area." I'm convinced, though, that this is the region of the brain where human traits such as grammar and what's vulgarly termed spirituality, our inexpressible feelings and longings, are hardwired. The machine, quite simply, gives this part of the infant brain, and its supposedly preverbal owner, a voice. Of course, it took time, quite a lot of money and elbow grease, and brain cells rubbing together, to bring the project to this stage of development. I'm working on designs for a model that could fit in a Snugli, provided the mommy or daddy's got a strong back.

HOWLER MONKEY: Which leads us to the controversy swirling around the manufacture – I think that's the right word in this case – of your daughter, Antonia. She's adorable, by the way.

DR MOSS HARTWIG: Here, why don't you hold her for a while? She's been staring at you. Do you have any children?

HOWLER MONKEY: We do not. That's an editorial *we*, of course. I'm still looking around. Playing the field. I'm only thirty-five and. . . .

DR MOSS HARTWIG: Well, I certainly hope that whatever you're about to hear won't influence you, one way or the other. [Laughs.] Look, she likes you. Sometimes she cries and squirms when someone she doesn't know handles her. Infants respond more to sound and smell than to visual stimuli. I doubt those big blue eyes of hers are focusing on us now. She's drawn to you on an animal level. Yes.

HOWLER MONKEY: A beautiful child. Congratulations. But the fact of her birth has caused certain accusations to be leveled against you: "child abuser" being among the mildest. It's been said that you and your wife consciously conceived Antonia in order to verify your theories and to test whether or not your machine works: is that true?

DR MOSS HARTWIG: Yes, sure it is. But what's wrong with that? Several years ago, a couple we know, some friends of ours, had a child with a serious medical problem; a life-threatening birth defect, to be frank. The condition was correctable, but it required a lengthy and extremely delicate operation. The donor of the organ that needed to be transplanted had to be a nearly exact genetic match; a blood relative; a twin, preferably. But there was no twin, and a donation by the parents was out of the question, if only for reason of scale. So they quickly got to work to produce another offspring, a girl, who, weeks after being born, donated one of her organs – the organ in question is dispensed in pairs – and saved her brother's life. No hoo-hah there, believe me. Even though the mean doctors cut the sweet little baby girl open like a chicken to harvest – that is the exact medical term – her living tissue. And she hadn't signed a donation form. If that same little girl had been born five months ago, instead of when she was – lovely, healthy little girl by the way, and devoted to her older brother – I could've strapped her into the Anthony and gotten her opinion on the matter. I have no doubt as to what she would have said, then. Now, of course, she says, "I was born to save my brother." And beams with happiness at the thought. [To his daughter.] What do you say, sweetie-pie? Shall we sit in the funny old chair and play at talking like the grown-ups?

HOWLER MONKEY: Before we begin, Doctor . . . the St Anthony Organ . . . I mean, its biomechanical interpreter, or brain-wave synthesizer or whatever you prefer to call it, is, aesthetically at least, an extremely pleasing object. One is drawn to it. One wants to touch and stroke it. Are you responsible for its design as well as its conception and operation?

DR MOSS HARTWIG: Oh yes, of course. I wasn't happy about the way the last piece wound up looking – nasty little octopus-cockroachy contraptions they are – but that arose from strict necessity, and anyway, since they're implanted, nobody has to see the damned things. But since the Anthony has to be so big at this stage, I wanted it also to be, you know, sort of magnificent. I guess that entails a degree of vanity.

HOWLER MONKEY: You garnered highly favorable reviews – your only positive press in this matter – from several avant-garde art publications. Gina Ashcraft wrote –

DR MOSS HARTWIG: Gina's a friend of mine. I blurt this out in the name of full disclosure. She flattered me by saying –

HOWLER MONKEY: You know Gina Ashcraft?

DR MOSS HARTWIG: Oh hell, yes. She's been to two of my balls . . . oh, hurh-hurh. I mean . . . I didn't want it to look like something that belongs in a hospital – phlegm-gray, drab, dull. And at the same time, I didn't want to hire, say, some design hotshot like Reny Fleur and then he gets all the glory for slapping together what's essentially a housing. There weren't to be any superfluous appurtenances on the Anthony, either: no sound effects, or light shows, or ergonomic dials and switches and knobs. So I followed my own aesthetic inclinations for the outward appearance of things. Which is something we physicians don't get to do all that often. I wanted the design to inspire joy too, because let's face it, a lot of the work I had to do to develop the Anthony was so lugubrious and depressing.

HOWLER MONKEY: What do you mean?

DR MOSS HARTWIG: Well . . . you try dissecting the brains of hundreds of cute little stillborn babies, and those horrid malformed monsters we're seeing in ever-greater numbers, and you'll get an idea. Which brings us back to Antonia. I mean, you can't go around sticking probes, however painless and harmless, into the brains of other people's healthy children, after all. They will not give you permission. Feel free to examine her; all over, if you please. Antonia is whole and unharmed. I would never, I assure you, do anything to cause her pain or discomfort or fear. She is my greatest creation, not this lifeless implement, this . . . this Byzantine household appliance. Go on, you may inspect her while I put the probes in place. It's all done with lasers and a process that I've termed *transubstantication*. Certain patents are still pending, so I regret I can't explain further. . . .

HOWLER MONKEY: God, even the electrodes are graceful, well-balanced little masterpieces. May I touch one of them?

DR MOSS HARTWIG: Certainly. Just don't point the lens directly at your eyes. Or Antonia's, or mine, please.

And they're not electrodes. But that doesn't matter. A kid in Long Island City makes them for me, to my specs.

HOWLER MONKEY: Were you surprised when your invention was selected to be shown at the Off-World Biennial?

DR MOSS HARTWIG: You mean, when no scientific convention or exposition would touch it with a ten-light-year pole? Yes, I was. But I'm not naïve. I think Gina Ashcraft may have had a hand in that business. I know she's on the Biennial Commission. She and I were once . . . shall we say, involved. And there are quite a few grateful wealthy breeders who became art collectors on my recommendation.

HOWLER MONKEY: And you're planning to transport the piece, your invention, by yourself, in a rusty, explosion-prone crate like the space shuttle. Why?

DR MOSS HARTWIG: Aesthetics, once again. I have an affinity for the ruinous. The *Tomorrowland* reminds me of the Taj Mahal. It's a funerary monument: a splendid, white, domed tomb, with all the mystery that implies. And it's an expression in stone of eternal love and longing. I'm retrofitting the vehicle with the latest quantum expanders and warp drives, but I'll be at the helm in my Hanuman costume. As we speak, tailors are crafting a space suit with eight sleeves.

HOWLER MONKEY: What's the question you wanted this machine to answer? What grand theory are you trying to formulate?

DR MOSS HARTWIG: Don't think of it that way: it makes no sense at all. Instead, look at the face of the baby you're holding. Your answer, the grand theory, is there. This is the last time you will see an infant in the way you're accustomed. Eyes wide, as though in wonder at it all, mouth slightly open, the sweet drool . . . everything is new for her. She is a mysterious creature, is she not?

HOWLER MONKEY: Or perhaps one devoid of mystery. Incapable of fending for herself. Entirely subject to the most primal urges.

DR MOSS HARTWIG: Yeah . . . okay, I'm turning it on now. Takes a minute or two to warm up. All the circuits and transubstanticators have to get to know each other all over again. What a bore.

HOWLER MONKEY: Doctor! Something's wrong with your daughter's eyes! I can see things moving inside them. They're flashing. This is weird. Oh my god, turn it off. Turn it off! I'm not ready for this shit!

DR MOSS HARTWIG: Relax. Everything's fine. What you're seeing is nothing new, believe me. It's like staring into the sun. You've been told it's bad for you, and it is. Now, this isn't bad for you, but it's disorienting in much the same way. In a moment or two, however, it will seem entirely natural and logical.

HOWLER MONKEY: I don't understand.

DR MOSS HARTWIG: Of course not. But don't worry. Relax your grip on the poor kid's arm a smidge. You like to have a forearm under your knees, don't you, Antonia? Elbow at your neck and a palm under your bottom. A nice comfy chair of flesh.

ANTONIA: It is reassuring to be held, yes. And it's interesting to see things from the point of view of those who support me. I want to look out, not always up, or in. The blurriness is not unpleasant. Voices are a comforting drone. I like the smell of this stranger-woman.

HOWLER MONKEY: Wait a minute. Her mouth didn't move.

DR MOSS HARTWIG: C'mon . . . she's not Mortimer Snerd. Imagine you've been in an iron lung for nine months, growing to fill your allotted space entirely. Imagine the discipline and the serenity of mind it takes to deal with the claustrophobia. Silence is the rule. She hasn't learned all the complicated muscle movements necessary for speech yet. But her brain is fully formed, hence the big head that's so endearing. You're hearing her brain speak. You wouldn't be upset, or skeptical, I think, if this were, say, an adult ALS patient, immobilized by the disease and seemingly dead, speaking through a brain-activated computer and speech synthesizer. The concept's the same, though my machine's significantly more advanced.

ANTONIA: Oh, he's ever so smart, is Dr Hartwig.

DR MOSS HARTWIG: Let's lay off the easy irony, shall we, sweetness? This nice lady has some questions she'd like to ask you.

ANTONIA: Would she take off her shirt first? Nice . . . soft . . . bigger than Mama. I can smell I'm not going to get anything good out of them, but still. . . .

DR MOSS HARTWIG: You don't mind, do you?

HOWLER MONKEY: This isn't some cheap pickup scam of yours, is it, Hartwig? I've heard things about you. If you want to see my tits, why don't you ask me?

DR MOSS HARTWIG: Babies like breasts. Everyone does. It's I who have agreed to talk with you today. Antonia hasn't, or not yet. Here, let me take her while you. . . .

HOWLER MONKEY: Oh, all right.

DR MOSS HARTWIG: If it would make you more comfortable, I could take off my shirt as well. Then we'd all be on an equal footing, as far as clothing's concerned.

HOWLER MONKEY: Doesn't matter. I'm not shy. This is for *Howler Monkey* after all, not *New Truth*.

DR MOSS HARTWIG: Why don't you begin? No x-rated questions, please – just kidding. Ask whatever you want. Antonia has nothing to hide. She likes you. Nice tits, by the way.

HOWLER MONKEY: Where have you just come from, Antonia? I don't mean Mommy's tummy or the room next door. I mean, before that. And what was it like there?

ANTONIA: Bright . . . bright . . . blindingly so. Hot. Crowded. Violent and rushed, but without pain. The violence and speed bring us all together, makes the heat that places us here. Before, there is no I, nor you, or even we. No bones separate our hearts and brains and souls. Babies making babies, without bodies, without making. Out there, in there, during there, we are sparks that fuse together, giving off light and heat. We are not consumed. We are multiplied without losing ourselves, our collective ourselves . . . and it's exciting.

HOWLER MONKEY: That's strange. I expected words describing blackness, peace, and nothingness.

ANTONIA: There's nothing wrong with being. With being something. With being one instead of another, or something else. Especially not now. Everything is given to me. All I have to do is cry out, or reach out, indicate somehow that I want – up to you to figure out what that is. Later, it'll be up to me. For a time. I understand that and do not fear.

HOWLER MONKEY: What do you want, Antonia?

ANTONIA: Since I am alive, I want to remain alive. It's stronger than I am.

DR MOSS HARTWIG: Do you mind if I ask her something? It just occurred to me. Antonia, my darling baby, as you know, we can choose to die. Some people claim we can even will it to happen without self-inflicted violence – meditate, concentrate on stopping the heart, stop breathing, darken the brain, deaden all the nerves. But can we choose to be born? And to whom? If not, who decides?

ANTONIA: As I told you, it's hot and exciting and confusing. There's a feeling of building-up, of speed and tension increasing, and then you and the other . . . suddenly, there is an other . . . the incredible brightness and heat that is the usual becomes warmth and quiet and darkness, with a rhythm to it. With this peace, we are lulled, stunned out of activity and brilliant expression. As to choice, no; it happens, or it doesn't. If not now, some other time. It's all the same.

DR MOSS HARTWIG: Do you love me, Antonia? Do you love Mommy?

ANTONIA: I'll learn, perhaps. Feed me. Keep me comfortable.

DR MOSS HARTWIG: [Laughs.] Isn't that horrible? I ask her that all the time and she keeps telling me the same thing.

HOWLER MONKEY: Have you been reincarnated, Antonia? By this we mean were you somebody else before you arrived here, now. An other, as you said.

ANTONIA: I know what reincarnation means, pretty lady. Yes . . . many others, so many. The heat and light cause this, this multiplication and expansion. But there isn't memory of it. I don't remember. He tells me that later there will be moments of recall, flashes of things already seen, lived. Have you noticed this?

HOWLER MONKEY: Yes, I have. Like, right now I think I must be dreaming. I've already had this dream.

ANTONIA: Yes. It all comes back. Sometimes the recall is happy, sometimes not. I have such feelings myself. I feel lonely even when there's someone present, touching me, admiring me, feeding me. The only explanation I can formulate is that it is nostalgia for the bright collective, for being a drop in the ocean, a droplet of vapor in a cloud in the sky, a flicker of a great flame. Consolation is the certainty that this state will be again, when I am summoned back, and you, to . . . where? And in what form? There is no telling, not that it makes the slightest bit of difference.

HOWLER MONKEY: Her vocabulary's prodigious. This makes me somewhat skeptical, Dr Hartwig.

DR MOSS HARTWIG: It's true that the machine is assisting her, up to a point. Her infant brain formulates concepts, some of them sophisticated to the point of being mystical and abstruse. The machine's task is to give verbal expression to these brain waves, the conceptual constructs and emanations. Her mouth, tongue, and vocal cords are undeveloped, have not been exercised, trained. Imagine you hadn't been able to say a word, had no external stimuli save the rush of blood in a mother's heartbeat for a period that seems infinite to the fetus; a lifetime would be the adult equivalent. What would your voice sound like then? Independent from what your brain might be desirous of expressing? Baby talk, or worse. Grunts. Meows. The damp barking of a catfish. To get back into it, she was talking about nostalgia for the orgiastic collective conflagration. Ask her about sex. Go on.

HOWLER MONKEY: What? Really? How can she know about penis and vagina stuff?

ANTONIA: No, there's none of that. Organs and arousal and functionality and fertility are for here, for this dimension. Here you've got one or the other, to varying degrees. I'm a girl, he tells me, a pretty little girl, but I can't imagine what that means. You are a pretty lady, she who feeds me is a pretty lady. He who interrogates me is a man. She tells me he's rich, so I mustn't cry. What I remember is constant crashing together, merging, fusing together and it changes everything and nothing and it doesn't matter but it feels wonderful. Fire, water, air, heavy matter – these things ecstatically moving, never stopping, until you're pulled out or choose to go and then all is stillness and blackness and rest and peace which inspires silence. But I don't want to talk about it anymore. It makes me sad, because. . . . [Her cry-baby sounds are echoed by the machine.]

HOWLER MONKEY: There, there, baby. I'm sorry. I didn't mean to upset you.

ANTONIA: Boo-hoo . . . abbasalonika . . . trains . . . asanisimasa . . . fish! Going into the tunnel now . . . skibble-a-diddle . . . snakes! Ca-ca. Pee-pee. Ma-ma! Da-da!

DR MOSS HARTWIG: Uh-oh! She does get tired easily. I always forget. Some of the things she says are so complicated and bizarre . . . that has to be a strain. Too bad we didn't have time to get into the State Tax Lotto numbers. Only a joke! Come here, darling. Daddy's sorry. There . . . off come these sticky, sparkly thingies, one by one, and this little piggie goes whee-whee-whee!

ANTONIA: Oral imperative! Metempsychosis. Mass psychosis. Onanism. Omphalos. Omnivorousness!

HOWLER MONKEY: Hey, wait! She's still talking, even without those electro-thingies on her.

DR MOSS HARTWIG: Oh no, that's just residual sparks of expression in the machine. Verbal backwash. There's still a partial erection after one blasts off the DNA, isn't there? Still some thunder after the storm's past. The machine's highly sensitive. But now it's time for pretty baby's nap. Or maybe it's her feeding-time. Ning! Basham! Boo-latta-why-oh! Ursula! Ursula, my dear? Will you please feed the baby? May we impose?

[A handsome, darkly tanned young man, kitted out in turban and sarong, enters the room. He is accompanied by a striking young woman dressed in Vietnamese ao dai. She has disfiguring scars on the left side of her face, which somehow only accentuate her beauty. Together, they remove Antonia. The baby's mother is making grandiose mommy-sounds in the background.]

DR MOSS HARTWIG: How silly of me. Shouldn't have her talking for more than ten minutes or so. You can ask her specific questions, at times. On other occasions, she'll insist that there's a war on, or that she is, in fact, a whale calf. I wish . . . I wish I had other neonates to talk to, just for comparison's sake. Double-blind testing and all that, you know? But it's astounding how fearful, how incurious parents can be. Maybe I ought to cart the Anthony down to the Ozarks, or western Pennsylvania. Offer them money to chat with their latest spawn.

HOWLER MONKEY: By the way, will you be taking Antonia with you to the Off-World Biennial?

DR MOSS HARTWIG: In the *Tomorrowland*? Are you

joking? Besides, she might be in the Interplanetary Academy by the time they get around to deciding where it's going to be held, and stop fighting about who gets to design the galleries and who gets the gift shop concession. Maybe I'll find some alien baby there, or along the way. An alien baby with more liberal, less fearful and superstitious parents. Or maybe someone'll drop dead at the Off-World and I'll do a corpse-miracle. That should get me some good reviews.

Hey, would you be interested in taking part in a little experiment? I've done it myself, but I have no way of confirming data; it's not strictly valid. I assure you there's no risk, nothing to fear . . . would you agree to a session with the Anthony? Just to see what happens?

HOWLER MONKEY: Oh jeez, I dunno . . . won't make me revert to some primitive state, will it? Can I put my top back on now? I mean, what if your wife comes in?

DR MOSS HARTWIG: Ursula's seen tits before, and anyway, two of these electro-thingies, as you so charmingly called them, would look nice on your coral-pink teats. . . . She doesn't understand me, you know. Never has. Please?

HOWLER MONKEY: Oh, all right. In the interests of science and journalism, I guess. . . .

DR MOSS HARTWIG: I found it rather pleasant, I assure you.

HOWLER MONKEY: Ooh! Tickles. Sparkles. Warm water . . . flowing. Flowing.

DR MOSS HARTWIG: Here, let me turn it up a trifle. It's fun, you'll see. Liberating.

HOWLER MONKEY: Wait a minute! No! Yes! Oh God, I'm so wet . . . fuck me! Fuck me! Ma-ma! Ca-ca! Ga-gaahh. . . .

What happened, basically, is this: I squealed and cried and thrashed around and wet and soiled myself. Thanks loads, Dr Hartwig, for not telling me about that part. It was only mortifying, though, when the Anthony was turned off and the transubstanticators were removed. What I recall – and the memory's fading, unfortunately – is the most wonderful, rushing, absolutely sexual energy and vitality of the Anthony-state. Myself letting go absolutely, in all ways, all directions: my identity as a self, an ego, being a woman, an intellectual *pornagrapheuse* (flatter, flatter) . . . gone! I'll say this: it was the biggest splashing orgasm I ever had.

According to the good doctor, the frictional interaction of sparks/charged particles/prospective souls is highly sexual in nature, and it is, he says, the elusive fusion furnace – the engine that drives the stars. He's convinced that Antonia's mother would benefit from interviewing her child about this, but Dr von de Gruft adamantly refuses. It's difficult for physics brains to take in the underlying mystical concept, apparently. Also, she will not agree to strap on the electro-thingies. As a woman, I recommend that she try it. Much better than any cheap sex-shop pocket-rocket.

I inquired whether the next phase of the Anthony's evolution might be a linkup with two adult subjects. Dr Hartwig expressed concern that spontaneous human combustion could occur. Well, I'm sorry to be saying this in print, Mossy-honey, instead of face-to-face in an intimate tête-à-tête, but I'm ready to burn up with you. Here on Earth, or in the *Tomorrowland*, or at the Off-World Biennial, or in the brightness beyond.

MY STORY

This mess began when I flew into Iraq on a Blackhawk helicopter operated by Halliburton/Time Warner, the media and war-services company. The behavior of the soldiers on board alarmed me. Vulgar slogans were written all over their helmets; you could hardly see the Nike insignias.

The flight over New Israel was uneventful. Excuse me, I meant to say occupied Basra. The Israeli invasion of southern Iraq in 2007, and their seizure of the Rumaila oilfields, was abhorrent. I should add that the American occupation of the Kirkuk fields – and the Russian invasion of the west of the country – are also illegal.

The chopper passed over Basra and headed toward Baghdad. The soldiers talked about the factions fighting over "Mogadishu-on-the-Tigris," as they called it. I believe one of the groups is backed by the Mossad, another by the CIA, another by the Iranians, and I'm not sure about the others. It reminded me of Somalia in the 1990s: a carrion country.

Thirty minutes later we landed at Kirkuk 69, the main American base. It is a very strange place. The soldiers carry whatever weapons they prefer; Uzis are their favorite. They have beards and wear T-shirts and don't bother saluting their officers, who don't seem to mind.

I was led to an air-conditioned tent that was the size of a ballroom, its floor covered with Persian rugs. I took off my boots and an Arab boy brought me a Pepsi, which has a sponsorship deal with the U.S. Army. A group of soldiers sat on pillows in a corner, playing cards and smoking hashish.

The commander, a certain Colonel Haight, was at the rear of the tent, sitting behind a desk, and he motioned for me to join him. He is about forty years old but still muscular, like a just-retired linebacker of the IBM Jets.

"Guggenheim guy, right?" he said, pointing a finger at me like a revolver. "Welcome to 69. Take a load off." He opened a folder. "Got the orders from my jackass bosses at the AT&T Pentagon. They want us to get the Vase of – what's it called?"

"Warka," I told him.

"Check. Vase of Burka. Where's this crockery? Jackasses don't say. In the north? Turks are genociding the Kurds again, so we're staying clear of that. In the south? Israelis might know but won't tell us unless we do something nice for them, like pretend they're not siphoning oil from our fields."

I explained that I had contacted Ibrahim Sadr, the son of Muqtadah Sadr, who was killed a few years ago by Spetznaz assassins employed by Yukos, the Russian oil company. Or maybe the hit was done by Green Berets working for Viacom/NASA, which was upset, according to a rumor I heard, that Sadr refused to authorize a Three Cloned Tenors concert in Babylon. Anyway, Ibrahim Sadr confirmed that he possessed the vase but said he might sell it to Osama bin Laden, who, he claimed, wanted to destroy it because it depicts human faces.

I don't know what you might have heard of my work, but it's simply not true that I intended to destroy the vase once I returned to America with it. Yes, several of my recent artworks involved the destruction of other artworks. I believe the world ignores art, or doesn't appreciate it sufficiently, so I decided, several years ago, that creating more of it would not draw more attention or appreciation to artistic works: only the destruction of artworks would do that.

Consider what happened after the Taliban destroyed the famous stone Buddhas at Bamian. The world was horrified, and the Taliban were out of power shortly afterward. Today the Buddhas are back where they were, reconstructed from the dynamited pieces, and tens of millions of dollars have been donated to preserve other works in Afghanistan; the country's forgotten and decaying antiquities are now getting their due.

I have not destroyed any important pieces. The Monet that I cut to bits in 2007, televised live, was the sort of minor work that museums store in their basements and never dust off for public viewing. You should know that the vast majority of artworks owned by museums are never displayed. I have not mentioned this before, but you should also know that the valuable works I have destroyed were not the originals, just copies; the real pieces are stored at my house in Woodstock. I would have done the same with the Vase of Warka. By pretending to shatter it, I would have helped Iraq by drawing attention to the Mesopotamian antiquities that are being destroyed in the ongoing chaos, and by men like bin Laden.

I am sorry for the digression. I told Colonel Haight that I needed to meet Sadr in Najaf. Sadr agreed to a $50,000 payment for the vase, plus 10,000 shares in the Guggenheim's upcoming IPO. He also wanted a seat on the board, but I explained that his followers might be displeased with the museum's racier exhibits, such as last year's very popular retrospective, "The Phallus: From Leonardo Da Vinci to Ronald Jeremy." Sadr withdrew his demand.

"I can't spare any men," Colonel Haight told me. "We're too busy running the oil fields and killing off the saboteurs hired by the Israelis or Russians or Chinese or God-knows-who. Just doing what it takes to keep the oil flowing to the homeland."

I reminded him that the recovery of the vase had the support of the board of directors of the AT&T Pentagon; as you may know, the secretary's wife is on the Guggenheim's board. Colonel Haight aimed a Glock at me and said, "You threatening me? I'm in charge, not the goddamn board. *Comprende?*"

I told him that I understood.

"Here's my plan," he continued. "You've heard about the Bruckheimer show, right? I'll send you out with one of the teams in a Humvee. Don't worry, the captain is one of my guys. The contestants aren't too bad, actually. I'll tell Sadr to send a technical here to escort you, you will all drive down to Najaf, meet Sadr, pick up your burka, and come back."

I was appalled. I had seen *Wargame Iraq* on television, but I assumed the missions were staged. I told the colonel that my recovery effort was unsuitable for a reality show. He fired a shot over my head and said, "You leave at 0400 tomorrow."

I showed up at the *Wargame Iraq* tent at 0330. The host, Geraldo Rivera, was distributing weapons to the cast members. There were seven of them, including Sammy, who told me that his conviction for killing his wife was overturned on appeal. There was another guy, Thomas, who was skinny and had an "Aryan Nation" tattoo on his arm. The only woman was Theresa, a professional bodybuilder who nearly broke a bone in my hand as she shook it and said, "They think this mission will kill in the global Nielsens." For emphasis, she pinched my nipple. I noticed that she had biceps to die for.

Geraldo gathered us around a map. As the cameras rolled, he explained that the distance to Najaf was 150 miles. The area we'd be traveling through was relatively calm; anarchy doesn't always mean violence, just the threat of it. The producers had already contacted the different warlords whose territory we would pass through; money had changed hands to reduce the odds of trouble. This seemed too good to be true, which it was.

"Some of you might have heard of the Al Jazeera show *Jihad Challenge*," Geraldo said. "One of their teams is going to try to stop you from reaching Najaf. They've been given the same weapons you have. It's you against them. Good luck, brothers."

At the entrance to Kirkuk 69 we met Sadr's crew, who were in a Toyota pickup with a 50mm machine gun mounted in its flatbed. A half-dozen fighters with rifles and grenade launchers were in the back. Their leader was named Salam. His left arm was a prosthetic limb missing two of its plastic fingers. Thomas said they had been shot off in a recent gun battle.

We had lipstick-sized cameras wired to our helmets, and our Humvee was outfitted with several more. Geraldo would follow us in a Humvee that had *Wargame Iraq* decals on its sides and a Pepsi sticker on its hood. He stood up through the gun turret in the roof, waving a pistol with which, I heard, he had mistakenly shot a twelve-year-old girl in Baghdad a few years earlier.

"Roll, roll!" Geraldo shouted, and off we went.

I knew this endeavor was unwise, but the Guggenheim had already agreed to sponsor my faux destruction work, and a contract had been signed with one of the television networks. I must emphasize that my mission was a just one. Failed states are incapable of preserving their historic treasures; they can't even preserve their roads. Provocative artistic works of the sort I intended are the best way to draw attention to this dismal situation. If Geraldo happened to be part of it, I couldn't do much about that.

The first ambush happened fifty miles outside Najaf. Dawn had just broken and the local gunmen were still asleep, as we expected. A cart pulled by a donkey was stretched across a bridge over the Euphrates, blocking both lanes. We slowed down, but before we could turn around we took fire from the *Jihad Challenge* contestants hiding behind the cart. I knew it was them because of the gold Al Jazeera insignia on their helmets.

Thomas was in the Humvee's turret and shot back with a large-caliber machine gun; the only casualty of his inexpert firing was the donkey, which bleated like a sheep as bullets rippled its hide.

Theresa and I jumped out and ran for a ditch as an RPG whizzed behind us. "Fast!" she yelled, spraying the bridge with her AK-47. I landed on the ground next to her, and she was already shouting into her walkie-talkie, "Geraldo, we need air cover! Now!"

"Roger that," Geraldo replied.

Geraldo's Humvee had pulled over a few hundred yards back, safe from attack because it flew the Fox Entertainment flag. As you know, the Geneva Conventions were amended in 2005 to provide immunity to personnel and vehicles involved in the production of entertainment programs in a war zone.

"But remember," Geraldo said, "you're allotted two air-support attacks on this mission, so you'll only have one left after this."

The *Jihad Challenge* team fell back before a squadron of Halliburton F-16s strafed the bridge. Theresa said we'd stay in the ditch for fifteen minutes, until the coast was clear, then move out again.

She smelled of desert and gunpowder. She put her hand on my cheek and said, "Don't worry, babe, we'll get through this." Her eyes were bloodshot with adrenalin. She lifted my helmet from my head and took off hers, putting her lips to mine with a kiss that felt like a breeze. I ran my fingers along her flexed bicep.

"Now," she whispered, "here."

She took off her fatigues and pulled down mine, straddling me as I lay on my back. I ran my fingers over her washboard abdomen and onto her silicone breasts. She cupped her hands around mine, tightening my grip. "Hard," she said. "I want to feel fear."

She guided me inside her and moved up and down,

like a hammer, in short bursts. She winced with each thrust. I grabbed her shoulders and rolled her onto the ground, onto her back, and went deeper still. "Shoot, as hard as you can," she urged. She wasn't talking about the Kalashnikov beside us.

When it was over she pushed me aside and pulled on her trousers. I noticed the cameras on our helmets, which were pointed at us, and she laughed. "You bet," she said. "Global audience. Better warn your mother."

As we crawled out of the ditch I saw Geraldo, back up the road, giving us a leering thumbs-up.

We continued south in our Humvee. The *Jihad Challenge* team tried to ambush us again, on the outskirts of Najaf. They were hiding in a grove of palm trees, but Salam had spotted them and opened fire. Before running away they got off a few shots, one of which hit Salam's prosthetic arm; his plastic hand shattered, splintering into a multi-edged dagger. Thomas laughed and called him "Salam Scissorhands."

We drove into Najaf, which was quiet. Sadr's headquarters was in an alley, not far from the shrine to Imam Ali. As we pulled up, Thomas scampered ahead and climbed onto a roof, to serve as a lookout. Theresa, with a Beretta in one hand and her AK-47 in the other, shouted at me to follow her. Sammy trailed behind, carrying a briefcase with the cash. The rest of the team set up a cordon along the alley.

There was no furniture in Sadr's office, just pillows on the floor and five plasma screens tuned to the BBC, Al Jazeera, CNN, Fox, and Nickelodeon. Sadr, who wore a red and white kaffiyeh on his head, stood up and shook my hand.

"I am glad to see you," he said. "You have brought the money, yes?"

I nodded toward Sammy, who raised the briefcase.

"Very good," Sadr said. "You do not mind if we examine it?"

"And the vase?" I replied.

Sadr motioned toward a wood crate in a corner of the room.

Sammy handed the briefcase to one of Sadr's assistants, who began feeding the bills into an automatic counter. As the notes whizzed through the machine, I pried off the crate's lid and pulled out the limestone vase. I shivered as I ran my fingers along the etchings of Sumerians offering gifts to the goddess Innin. The vase was 5,000 years old and in perfect condition.

I heard a commotion outside as the last bills were fed into the counter. Suddenly the doors opened and several Gurkhas burst through. In a split second one of them wrapped his arms around Theresa's head and snapped her neck; another one slit Sammy's throat with a kukri, the traditional Gurkha knife.

They didn't threaten Sadr, encircled by bodyguards. It was a standoff until a Gurkha shouted, "Clear!" and several more entered, followed by a tall, slightly stooped Arab man wearing a white turban. I recognized him immediately, and so did Sadr, who stepped forward, through his bodyguards.

"Osama," he said, "this is an outrage. I decided to sell the vase to the Guggenheim man, not you. You had your chance."

Bin Laden replied in a soft voice, "I have reconsidered. The infidel museum is paying $50,000, right?"

"And 10,000 shares in its IPO."

"I will pay $100,000."

Bin Laden then turned toward the door. "Bring in the infidel journalist," he ordered.

Several more Gurkhas entered, and behind them was Matt Drudge, the CNN anchorman, followed by two camera crews.

I realized what was happening. Halliburton/Time Warner, which owns CNN, knew of my mission and didn't want Fox to get the scoop of retrieving the vase: they brought Drudge to Iraq and enlisted the support of bin Laden.

"The vase is mine," Drudge said, stepping toward me. "This puppy is going to corporate headquarters at Columbus Circle. The Guggenheim can take a hike."

I looked at Sadr.

"Very sorry," he said, "but $100,000 is, how shall I say, a finer price."

Drudge grabbed the vase and turned to one of his cameras.

"This is Matt Drudge, reporting live from Najaf, with a world exclusive. I have in my hands the –"

Just then, in the vestibule outside the office, I heard a familiar voice shouting, "Let me in, asshole, don't you know who I am?" The doors opened and Geraldo entered, waving his pistol, followed by Salam and three camera crews.

"What the hell is going on?" Geraldo yelled. "Drudge, you cocksucker, that vase is ours."

"No it's not," Drudge replied.

"Yes it is," Geraldo insisted.

"No. Get out of my live shot."

"Fuck you. You're in my live shot."

Geraldo reached for the vase. In the ensuing tussle both men fell to the ground and the vase rolled to my feet. Salam lunged at Drudge and swiped his face with his prosthetic scissors. Drudge howled, even though the cuts were superficial.

A furious shout froze everyone.

"Stop this madness!" It was Osama. "The vase doesn't belong to any of you." He glared at the journalists. "Mr Drudge, Mr Rivera, you are my prisoners." He turned toward a back door. "Peter, you may enter now."

Peter Arnett stepped into the office, followed by four camera crews. Arnett was fired by NBC during the war of 2003, when he made statements critical of the American government. As you know, he soon moved to Dubai, and after several years of obscurity he became the host of *Jihad Challenge*.

He turned to one of his cameras.

"This is Peter Arnett, live from Najaf, where the *Jihad Challenge* team has triumphed, capturing the spies from *Wargame Iraq* along with Matt Drudge, the Zionist from CNN. The American plot to steal the Vase of Warka has been foiled."

It made perfect sense. The money that bin Laden would get from CNN was less valuable than the prestige he would gain from preventing the vase being taken away and arresting the men who wished to do so. And the ratings for Al Jazeera, in which bin Laden recently acquired a forty percent stake, would be quite good.

I did not resist as a Gurkha took the vase from my hands and handed it to bin Laden. Now that he has left the room, my fate is in your hands, viewers of Al Jazeera. I ask for your mercy as you decide, in your voting on the *Jihad Challenge* website, which one of us Americans will be executed.

THE REAL THING

Determinate 90210 is where it lies, naked and beaming, with a sickening psychedelic voracity that was blackened by an unknown source sometime in its early final moments. It is the perceived cause of the retroendless tangled mess that we now find ourselves eternally experiencing in 2304. My glamorous task, as a renowned HAIRologist (Higher Art InterReceptology) is to transfer it to determinate 4330 for a rare triennial.

I have been obsessed with this particular piece of production for quite some time. It's categorical distinction as ART came later than expected. However, once the stasis was obtained, I have worked steadily to extract an authentic signature for the creator. I have located a promising sequence of ES and OS (in the same determinate, 90210) that are generally believed to be significant. However, there is much speculation that it may be dated incorrectly. This is largely due to its labor-intensive, rather compulsive properties, and its employment of techniques considered antiquated even at the time of its creation. The production has been the subject of countless, ludicrous conjectures, which were mainly formulated using the cannotquitpoststructuralist model. Thankfully, a new set of superstructures has risen and

HAIRology has achieved its rightful position as a respected model.

The production, which is fondly referred to as "Swarzkopf," became infamous in the 1990s. It has been reported, by Codependents intradecade10 and mini-spin6month, to have elicited at that time a serious set of circuitous, irreversible tremors. Chemical analysis of the production has described the phenomenon as a blackout. This analysis, of course, provided us with our first glance at the reflected formula transmittal: Control Hair = Control Life. Thus successfully awakening what had been – so determinedly and so long ago – put to sleep by its creator. Thereby elevating Hair to a status of unfathomable omni-import. We all have it (referred to commercially as proteinconduits) . . . to varying degrees . . . I myself am blessed with a thick coif, the color of a smooth rainbow-rinse.

Swarzkopf and I are beginning the transferal process, a delicate and arduous procedure. I have been expending significant energy learning a set of intricate commands that will unlock certain principles and allow them to travel, via my proteinconduits, to determinate 4330. I find the initial commands a bit confusing. My favorite might be CUT THE CRAP BITCH, or, YOU'VE GOT A FRIEND, followed by BUNGLE IN THE JUNGLE. I haven't the foggiest idea what triggers what and I would feel better had there been more sufficient interpretations at my disposal. Nevertheless, Swarzkopf and I are entering the second level of the process with a rapport exceeding trust.

I suppose I should explain that my proteinconduits are exceptional. They are of the E-glass (Electrical-glass) variety, which is of a lime-alumina borosilicate composition with low soda content. Stronger modulo-glasses exist, but they tend to overheat and become limp. They are, in my opinion, too fancy and complicated. Mine are of fairly original technology, and have a great capacity to throb and spurt without much coaxing. In transferal, molten glass is allowed to flow from my heated protein-conduit reservoir into an array of small orifices or "bushings." The melt is attenuated into a filament by drawing the molten material through the bushings at high velocity. Once the material solidifies the transferal may safely occur.

I anticipate eight more command sequence levels before entering wholly unmapped territory with Swarzkopf. No one has ever transferred Swarzkopf and because of its volatile behavior, I can hardly assume anything. I – and the HAIRologist community – are hoping that through this transferal, it may be possible to deduce the signature of the production as singular and unique. We hope that I will connect and dot sufficiently the OS and ES. Quite honestly, we are motivated by our need to ascribe blame for our condition to one individual. It isn't that we have it so bad, it's nice to have hair again after years of not being able to replicate it, but in the race to regain hair we simply missed the possibility to reverse the cycle, and are trapped in the minispasms that Swarzkopf unleashed.

In short . . . we can't shake the shag.

I'm back to entering sequence six and am experiencing some turbulent exchanges with Swarzkopf. It began with the command NAKED CAME THE STRANGER and grew intensely with FUZZY SISTER HAIR, subsiding with LIE. Reviewing this has led me to no conclusions. It may well be that RIDE THE TIGER was important as well. The turbulence was not entirely unpleasant.

Sequence seven brought some very unexpected visual apparatus, nothing dangerous, just some flowers and curvy lines. I will try to look up varieties of plants, and measure thickness and gestural line content after I finish the transferal. I am becoming very fond of Swarzkopf.

We are now approaching the perimeters of the known sequences. Eight is proving very pleasurable, lots of roundness and blackness precipitated by the command sequence BUFFY GO HUMP TWAT. Unfortunately SPLIT THE SCENE has spun me into a continuous roving subphase and I am starting to worry about my reinforcements. They have always been supple and loose – desirable properties because they can easily be shaped to meet sharp single or double curvatures, but for some reason they are proving too specific. I decide to switch to woven roving, which is a more attractive reinforcement subphase. It is balanced, unidirectional, and good for warp. I'm really floating now. My proteinconduits are like spaghetti and the blackness is rich and thick. The current warp direction is giving way to a kind of suspension, which results in an unexpected monotone flip. There is also some atmospheric threat, which is causing a ringlet stall.

I am receiving no new command signals from my prompters, but I should probably dream up some to get things rolling. There really isn't anything dangerous about this stall, but my desire is building. I am struggling to be disciplined and patient; the anticipation is daunting. I am afraid, and Swarzkopf is not helping. The stillness is deafening. I am desperate now. Confused, I plan to use a chemical enhancer to provoke my protein-conduits into new patterns and reinforcements. I am hoping for an intensely thick, tight, spiral-frizz formation referred to as an "A-Fro." It intensifies all stimuli points and is entirely electric. It is working for me, I am fully charged, but Swarzkopf isn't allowing connection, I'm not getting any light exchange. This poses a difficulty for my analysis, but I am trying to think of the darkness as potential.

I must invent something now.

I must invent something now.

I must invent something now.

I must invent something now.

I must invent something now.

I must invent something now.

I am fully charged, but Swarzkopf isn't allowing connection.

I must invent something now. I must invent something now. I must invent something now. I must invent something now. I must invent something now. I must invent something now.

I must invent something now.

I am fully charged, but Swarzkopf isn't allowing connection, I must invent something now. I am fully charged, but Swarzkopf – *now*! – isn't allowing connection.

I must invent something now. *Now*. Oh god, holy shit!

Ohhhh. . . .

Swarzkopf is releasing some bits. The first perceptible reference comes in as SAM SLEEPS.

My translation follicles tell me this could be about "Son of Sam" or Saul Bellow's Arthur Sammler, pinned and brandished with the unanswerable might of an immense penis.

TAXI DRIVER is next.

Time sensors reveal this as NYC, 1976. I have no way to assemble the references while in transferal, but I am capable of a silk response reflex.

I intuitively venture response commands, RAPE ROBBERY MURDER. Still only blackness: no reciprocation from Swarzkopf. I am wondering if I missed my chance by passively receiving bits from Swarzkopf. Is this a stylistic decoy or is there really something there? Oh shit, intense light is producing supermagnitudinal amorphicolor and I'm feeling a chemical burn on my proteinconduits. It's splitting the end-sensors and I am in need of a Flexrinse in the worst way – or maybe a Pantone protein enhancer. I am getting bored. The psychotropic Pharmakon relay system could help here because the usual linear male pattern baldness recognition circuit is not allowing forward thrust and my throb-and-spurt mechanism is becoming clogged. I issue the command ENDLESS LOVE, Swarzkopf issues ENDLESS SUMMER. I respond with STYLE WARS, Swarzkopf with WILD STYLE. ZORRO. BLOOMBERG. EGG. GOT ANY EGGS. LOOKING FOR MISTER GOODBAR. FARRAH FAWCETT. I am annoyed about Farrah because it doesn't have an O or an E just RS and TS. I resort to the risky procedure of expelling most of my coif. I must create possibilities. EE. EEC. EEG. Abbreviations for: Electrical Engineer, European Economic Community, and Electroencephalogram. Meaningless to me . . . I'll sort it out later.

Swarzkopf is trying to send an afterimage. This is seriously fucked! No! No image please! To counter inevitable image overload, I release a vile 3D form with sensual properties, an old trick, but I am desperate. Swarzkopf is sending an image of Warren Beatty!

Swarzkopf is really sick, even evil. My medical implant sensors are revving up and signaling severe hair-loss symptoms in Swarzkopf. Diagnosis: anorexia or compulsive abuse syndrome – the result of twisting, rubbing, or pulling. The poor fuck is a waxer and plucker! I make a note that no depilatories have been found here.

My sympathy busters are kicking in, which is not abnormal. I decide to be a little more specific with my impulse commands and whisper TAB PINK DIET. That gets Swarzkopf all excited, and I am feeling hope for the first time since sequence eight began. GIVE ME AN E. Swarzkopf answers: no e. I try: GIVE ME AN O. YES. THERE ARE TWO OS IN THE PUZZLE. VANNA WHITE. ARNOLD SCHWARZENEGGER. Swarzkopf is blocking now. I reverse the forming sequence and access the sympathy busters again; they suggest that I try a configuration-construction scenario. It is generally known that architecturally constructed space is essential for forced meaning exchange. The last known configuration was in the already impure salon form called "Barmacy," a combination of bar, pharmacy, and beauty salon. Neopostmoderncapitalism has a nauseating effect on me, but I am encouraged by the possibility of the little liquid curl a stiff Jameson would offer to my endings. Who knows, maybe Swarzkopf is into white lines? I invite Swarzkopf to Barmacy, NYC, 2002. If I'm lucky the local white line guy will give us a Pharmakon thrust. I give in to Warren, and Swarzkopf seems stimulated. We begin sucking and snorting. It is not entirely unpleasant. Swarzkopf is in heaven. I am trying to play down my impatience and the Jameson is helping. All in all, whiskey is still one of the better enablers.

It is common, but not mandatory, to describe architectural/interior design as perceived in the configuration-construction scenario. Essentially, Swarzkopf and I are in a long street-level shot-barrel series of half-rooms. The rooms are lined with the '50s hair dryers so beloved by the beehive set. The liquid and chemical bars are pure scummy smoked wood. Swarzkopf has opted for a vinyl turquoise dryer-lounge with tiny Buddhas embossed in bronze woven threads; I am in a pink-and-gold glossy glitter vinyl version. We continue to suck and snort. All of a sudden, Swarzkopf pulls a freak move and extracts a bronze thread from one of the Buddhas' noses and starts to cover it with KY. Swarzkopf slowly inserts the thread into my perfectly shaped rainbow proteinconduits. Not a wholly unpleasant sensation. Swarzkopf is now barking certain full sentences. My translation follicles are over-secreting, trying to derive meaning from what seems to be pure diplomaticspeak. I want to respond. I can't wait for cues from my oily follicles. I venture PERFECT TEN, followed by YES. Swarzkopf continues pulling threads off the Buddhas' noses and lubricating them with full compulsive rigor. This behavior and minute detailing is simply hideous. I attempt distraction with DADDY DADDY O. Swarzkopf replies: OH DADDY. Enough! With a sweeping entangle I engulf Swarzkopf in a Hirsutism hug, the likes of which would give any HAIRologist a bad case of alopecia areata. The Hirsutism hug is a strictly forbidden analytic method. I risk my great reputation to use it here. Honestly, I cannot help it; I am confused, repulsed, and frustrated. Scenario sensors are convincing me that I did it because of the timeriff warptide that Swarzkopf inhabits and unleashes. It is clear I must get out of the architectural construction configuration. I have to leave Barmacy!

I access determinate V5L 4G9 for more imagination. I have never utilized this source but have been told it is where x originated – x being the only revolutionary position against Swarzkopf. Unfortunately, I have overstepped the procedure and I am in triple-x. But Swarzkopf seems to be amused about something here. My proteinconduits are feeling exceptional and, with a little isopropyl pomade, Swarzkopf's gentle rubbing contractions on the lower glans of my proteinconduits are greatly enhanced. Swarzkopf, sliding down an inch or so at a time, is slowly lifting the beautiful blackout Caress layer with a firm but sensitive circular motion. It occurs to me at this point, for a fleeting second, that the rich blackout Caress is the very desire of the production's creator, but I cannot sequence anything. This is the moment I have been waiting for, but I am completely overcharged. Swarzkopf continues slowly, slowly, squeezing a little harder, a little harder. The rubbing motions are killing me, the temperature is too high, I can't freeze-frame for transferal. Oh no. Oh, no. Oh, oor, oorrrebeeeeeeek! Swarzkopf is shuttering, pleased and powerful now, and continues to slide down each proteinconduit gently, causing the conduit walls to contract with long, slow compressions. Swarzkopf and I lock into another Hirsutism hug and at this Celsius the explosion is inexplicable. I feel responsible for destroying Swarzkopf as we burst into a thousand bits of rainbow schuppen-dust. The colors are intense. I think I can bring this all back together and make the delivery in time for the triennial – if I can bring the temperature down and pull a deadening RetroResyncManeuver. The RRManny (as it is referred to by the heinous group that delivered it to the Southland) will kill anything, especially desire. It is irresistibly easy, lazy, always effective, and completely subjective. I am loath to employ it. I desperately wish the blackout Caress technique had been established and perfected, so I could stall effortlessly. My status as a respected HAIRologist is completely on the line here. I think Swarzkopf set me up for this. This is exactly the locus of power in Swarzkopf. I am not capable of distinction. I am now indistinguishably connected to all before the blackout. I will be swallowed by images, images of large throbbing penises and hairless, juicy cunts, chopped and cropped forever.

"MADAME DU BARRY, C'EST MOI"

Our man felt tired, but not really exhausted. It was the feeling that comes before true exhaustion, in which the need for relief and distraction is combined with indeterminate excitation. When he became aware of this state of mind he consulted the information terminal on the nail of his left index finger to select the appropriate stereotypical fiction character for the situation. He chose "private detective," a picturesque example from the mid-twentieth century that was subject to periodic revivals and thus relatively easy to absorb, and incorporated some basic mannerisms and emotional predispositions inherent to the character. Even without loading the dose, he began to feel enigmatic and universal.

He looked over to the other side of the street and an aroma of sensual expectation drew him into a recently opened voice bar about which he had registered a number of positive references. The establishment's quick success in an area of heavy competition was due to the quality of its new line of voice creams that enabled rigorous separation of the different vocal emission poles, ensuring the specificity of their relationship to different areas of the body. That old, unpleasant feeling of not knowing whether one is speaking with the voice implanted in the nipple or the shoulder blade was thus avoided.

This week the bar bore the façade of a traditional Irish pub whose aesthetics, light, and characteristic smells extended into the reception room. Here, the profile of an ideal assistant could be designed using a simple body-simulation device, while the physical body could be produced from a menu containing thousands of aesthetic features. The menu, so strange and enjoyable to use, was organized as a food menu that allowed the wildest fusions of taste, according to a combinational logic that recalled the ancestral culinary traditions of primitive California.

He could only smile when he generated a Franco-Arab whose long and ostentatious black beard was joined to the pallid and discolored aspect usually associated with representations of the sort of creatures that had once inhabited legendary Paris. To complete the picture our man added bristly red hair, but the final image was so implausible that he decided not to produce the body.

After a few other inconsequential attempts he ended up choosing the body of an Australian swimming champion from the Olympic period. For the hair he picked an ineffable very pale blond tone, halfway between "strawberry blond" and "cotton candy." For the eyes he opted for the Liz Taylor model, based on a mythic being that many called the Mother of All Mothers: she was still a major presence in the Carnival parades that left Beijing each week and ended with great fanfare in the holy ruins of Las Vegas after circling the Old World three times. For lips he chose without hesitation the Marilyn model; the label was associated with the name of a person who was also known as the Last First Lady, though nobody knew why. Finally, for skin tone he chose a Caribbean brown that had been in fashion since the restoration of a small island recently found adrift in an obscure chasm of the primitive oceans. It was called Cuba-on-the-Rocks and had been made into a sort of tropical garden/beach which became very popular after it was set in the third ring of the multimedia dome covering the vast Arctic pools. Every Sunday afternoon visitors laughed uproariously when the awkward hologram of the Commander (the Beast of Beard and Beret, as the children called him), got up to do his irresistible dinosaur dance routine.

When the selection of the menu items was finished, the ideal assistant was embodied and presented his greetings; with an encouraging grin he directed our man to the room where the voice creams would be applied.

Once the options of a sexual nature had been rejected, it was decided that what was most appropriate for our man would be an assortment of voices from the politico-cultural sphere, those most able to provide simultaneous gradual physical relaxation and light mental agitation.

The assistant undressed our man, directed him to a room barely illuminated by a subtle installation of stars in a distant sky, and laid him down on an immaterial total immersion bed. The voices were applied to the left nipple, the right palm, the right thigh, the left wrist, and along a slow circulation path around the neck. Our hero let himself be enveloped by the multiple caresses of voices that tried to lull him or attract his attention. The symphony of voices was marvelous, yet thanks to the new and perfected technologies it was also possible to differentiate them.

The voice from the right palm seemed to be that of an artist and ceaselessly complained about tiresome injustices. Around the neck a group of teenagers belted out a nice but not very exciting tune. The right thigh voice insisted on criticizing all the other voices and became so disagreeable that it had to be erased. The imperturbable left wrist alternated bucolic poems with revolutionary anthems. But eventually it was the left nipple that almost exclusively captured our man's attention.

The feminine voice projected a sensual heat, with a slight acridness and very mysterious echoes. It spoke of an intricate police plot that put it in a very dangerous situation. At the same time it described a valuable artistic treasure it wanted to show our man if he was willing to follow it to a more private and exclusive space. Lured on by this double appeal of danger and beauty, our man canceled the bar on the command panel set in his right thumb and let himself be transported by the voice to a transparent pink bed, vaguely suspended in a dark red-toned room illuminated by light golden dust.

The pink bed continually changed form according to the voice: at one moment it appeared to be a traditional bed, only to change into a convulsively moving ball of yarn that totally covered our hero and made him turn and move in all directions, but without ever losing his comfort or balance. A few moments later the bed began to move in a way so insinuating that it made inevitable a formal transformation – increasingly visible – of our hero's physical condition. The transformation evolved toward achievement of a sexual relationship with a partner he couldn't identify as other than the bed itself, but which nevertheless continued to provide the physical responses, positional variations, and small resistances and abandon that lead to full sexual satisfaction.

Although he hadn't heard her since changing spaces, our man never doubted the identity of the voice that inhabited the bed. After a comfortable pause, and very polite silence, he heard it resume its story with a small and hopeful sigh. The voice, now more at ease in the privacy of its own space, said it was one of the last self-sustained and self-renewed sentence production poles that could be classified in the mythology section of the arts. Almost all the other poles were extinct, only able to produce repetitions or chance combinations from a relatively limited number of overused phrase-blocks, some of which were in the process of disintegrating. The situation was alarming, though there was hope for salvation.

The story began with an acquisition, at a time now unknown, of the production code corresponding to the name of an artist. The code was enclosed in a capsule whose possession enabled production and reproduction of the respective artworks.

The voice had bought the code from the moribund echo of an old art critic, when the latter decided to exchange his sentence production matrix for a hat collection, by means of which he could become King of Human Cats, in the wake of one of those historical *volte-faces* not worth going into here.

The transaction was accomplished by a group of three underground lawyers, two of whom were found dead soon after the deal went through. Sometime later the images generated by the code began to have problems: it became increasingly difficult to produce new works by the artist, or reproduce existing ones, even though the artist had died only a few hundred years ago.

Now it was almost impossible to see the images remaining from the works, even though they were kept in optimal conservation conditions. The financial losses resulting from this problem were enormous, and for this reason the owner had passed over to voice condition and let herself be applied as a cream in voice bars, in order to try to find a user who could help her. The images' situation was increasingly precarious; the bluish liquid that protected them was becoming more and more expensive and the window for action was shrinking.

As the story filled up with details and antecedents our hero let himself drop into a pleasurable sleep-like lassitude through which only a few echoes of the complex intrigue reached him. But he was shaken out of this state when the voice turned up the volume and practically threw him out of the pink bed, insisting that he had to visit the gallery on the other side of the Polished Black Glass Gate. There he would find what remained of the artworks' images, suspended in a light blue liquid within a huge transparent aquarium.

Our hero was called upon to play the role of his hero character.

As soon as he looked at the Polished Black Glass Gate he was met and immobilized by a practically invisible human silhouette, which moved like the image of a ghost on the gate's surface and issued a humid smoke that gave him the shivers. The Shade said it didn't want to hurt him. Rather, it wanted to warn him of the danger he was in and of the sinister intentions of the voice that had drawn him there, called Mega-Megera, an age-old art collector – nobody could figure out why she was still alive. The Shade said it was the ghost of the third lawyer and that Mega-Megera had forced the old critic (who was now King of Human Cats) to give up his valuable code and had murdered the two other lawyers who had helped him in the operation. The Shade had only escaped because at the last moment it had fled to subterranean territory. It warned our hero that if he wasn't careful he would meet the same fate as the previous accomplices, and suggested that they deal with the problem together and escape from the curse of Mega-Megera. Besides this, it intimated that resolving the problem of the images' gradual extinction would be impossible without its help. Without waiting for an answer the Shade drew back with a chuckle, in a blast of icy smoke.

Our man looked ahead and saw the aquarium full of a bluish liquid and moved directly toward a transparent ladder whose rungs became illuminated by white neon lights as he climbed. He arrived at a crystal board covered with rainbow reflections that hovered above the aquarium and undulated like a flying carpet. Our hero, who had remained conveniently naked since he had lain down in the voice bar, hopped up and down half a dozen times on the crystal board, did two or three handstands, exercised and massaged his arm and leg muscles, closed his eyes, and, with Olympic perfection, dove into the aquarium.

When he opened his eyes again he was in the midst of an infinite blue, though it wasn't a liquid space like that of the ocean or a pool. He was not in water or any other liquid. It was a dry, cool space and he felt drawn to look toward the blue-encircled horizon – blue every which way. It was the blue air that kept him suspended in equilibrium, as if the very blue was floor, ceiling, and single endless horizon.

He gave himself over entirely to contemplating and enjoying the blue. He became increasingly sleepy and the blue got darker and darker until he found himself sitting in the middle of a very dark chamber lined with blue crushed velvet.

Short flashes of strong light shooting out in different directions produced a strobe effect that intermittently lit up images which he tried to distinguish from the dark blue of the velvet. It seemed he could make out a hint of country vegetation, a lock of blond hair, a pink face, an abrupt gesture, and a heart pang, all wrapped in a wave of green shades. But this was only for brief snatches. Everything led back to the heavy comfort of the blue velvet and our hero returned to the aquarium's surface, where the crystal carpet was waiting, invitingly.

The voice that had brought him there and which was again lodged in his left nipple returned to say that there was no time to lose.

This week the culmination of the Carnival parade due to take place in the holy ruins of Las Vegas included a major archaeological exhibition of primitive artistic codes, sponsored by the Grand Legion of Crystal Carpets, which had committed itself to restoring all the codes in the exhibition.

The grand Carnival parade was to pass by within three minutes; two of the parade's top attractions and exhibition curators, the Mother of All Mothers and the Last First Lady, had agreed to add the monumental blue-filled aquarium to their carriage in the great orbital Carnival train.

The only thing that had to be done to let the train pass by and to join it was to destroy the Polished Black Glass Gate. For this a diamond bullet was needed, shot from a silver pistol hidden in the rim of the crystal board. Our hero had no trouble finding these items, but he had only just aimed the pistol at the gate when the Shade reappeared, emitting a jet of icy flame. It said that without its presence the artist's name would be forever extinguished, because during the transaction it had kept the silver oval capsule containing the original author creativity code delivered by the old critic; it had given Mega-Megera a virtual image replica with a short expiration term whose efficacy had almost come to an end. The Shade slid into the aquarium and with another icy blast melted the Polished Black Glass Gate. Our hero concealed the pistol again as the crystal carpet spun rapidly upward, dragging the blue aquarium with it. The group took off in dizzy vertical flight, finally coming up close to a huge golden platform lit by neon lights of all colors, and covered by millions of creatures that shook to the rhythm of a frantic music.

A large door opened and a ramp was lowered, onto which the crystal board landed. A machine raised the large aquarium. It was carefully placed onto some rails that led it into an enormous warehouse where it was placed amid hundreds of objects of the most varied sizes, all enshrouded in black cloths. According to the signs on the cloths the objects were meant for the grand archaeological exhibition.

Before he could take in more details of the place, our hero, still lying on the crystal board afloat in the aquarium, had his vision horizon obscured by a thick black cloth. The only images that reached him were the rainbow emanations from the board. His feelings were fully absorbed by the sound produced by the creatures he had seen when he had arrived. Even so, he occasionally felt and heard a distinct and disturbing wheeze that he knew came from the Shade – now somewhere in the aquarium.

Suddenly the music stopped and a loud noise was heard, accompanied by a wash of light so intense that it penetrated the cloth. The sound of pulleys, chains, and elevators became louder and louder, as if gigantic machines were getting underway, until the aquarium jerked violently and began to rise quickly, as if sucked along a ramp. And things began happening as soon as it started to move.

The black cloth came off and fell apart in the air. The frantic cries and applause now obeyed a regular and cadenced rhythm, both exciting and scary. Our hero got up onto the crystal board and found himself suspended high up; at his feet was a compact crowd that didn't stop moving. He thought it must be the people watching the culmination of the Carnival parade. It seemed to him that for the time being he was the only object that was being presented in the exhibition. He raised his arms and noted that the crowd accompanied his movements with applause. He noticed that his body glimmered as if it were covered in gold. And at that moment he felt an icy breath that stuck to his skin and which in a few seconds rendered him totally immobile.

The Shade that had inhabited the Polished Black Glass Gate was now moving around him at incredible speed, shutting him into a sort of icy vortex shaped like a spiral web. Our hero, frozen and still, felt he was on the brink of losing consciousness when a wave of heat from his left nipple gave him back the energy and ability to move. He began to kick out in all directions, twirling round and round. The crowd shook even more and applauded his increasingly fast movements. Strong impacts and icy jets from his almost invisible opponent hit him relentlessly, obliging him to bend over, lose his balance and get down on his knees. Finally, as if he were carrying out a rehearsed movement, he stopped, lay down on the board, and didn't move for several seconds. Then, with the crowd in tense expectation, he got up with an acrobatic leap, brandishing the silver pistol that had been hidden in the board's rim. He fired a single shot and felt a last aggression, more violent than all the others, hit him square in the mouth. Then he heard a terrifying roar and saw the Shade shatter like glass, crash, and fade out, just before falling onto the crowd. He again felt hot and vigorous; he heard the delirious crowd and noticed he was still standing on the crystal board afloat in the big aquarium, which, seen from above, now seemed to have the size and appearance of a richly decorated interior.

He brought his hand to his mouth and realized that his lips were bloody. He felt the blood running down his chin and cupped it in one of his golden hands. In the blood he found a small silver oval capsule, the size of a nail from the little finger.

At that very moment another black cloth dropped down on him and the aquarium. At the same time a breathtaking, rapid descent vertiginously transported him to a dark and quiet place where he finally came to a stop. He could see or hear absolutely nothing.

He realized that the small silver capsule was still in his hand and with a little pressure from his fingers he opened it in the middle; inside was a light and luminous golden dust that our hero applied to his mouth, where he immediately stopped feeling any traces of blood.

Slowly, very slowly, the morning dawned around him. He saw he was inside a richly decorated room. He looked to his left and the growing light enabled him to pick out among the blue skies, green breezes, and soft treetops a pair of enamored youths looking at a letter, and another boy who was offering a girl a flower. Yet another boy with a showy pink shirt leapt out from a stairway and surprised a girl sitting at the foot of a statue. He looked right and saw that a smiling girl standing among bunches of flowers and fruit was placing a wreath of flowers on the head of a boy sitting at her feet, while an artist watched them. As the light revealed the room, he realised he could give life, color, and movement to all these scenes and characters.

He looked ahead and saw tree branches swaying outside, beyond the windows. He looked at a mirror and began to see the outlines of a friendly figure take shape, as a very familiar voice whispered in his ear the title of this story.

THE DAEMON CURATORUM

To the south of our borders, between the great fortress of Wouw and the western sea, lies the desert island called Zeelandis. Zeelandis has not always been a desert or even an island. A few centuries ago there had been lush forestland here, populated with ravenous trees that snared travelers and kept them as slaves bound in their roots. Flocks of rotting feathered things gathered thick enough to turn the sky black. But the jungle, that huge slab of hungry life, had fled south and east, toward Gandis and the Twerpian lowlands, cramming itself onto the precipitous ledges of the broken peninsulas, leaving behind utter desolation.

The ground it left behind was so dry it had petrified and cracked in the heat. The desert was a flat sheet of hot sandy-colored rock. Sometimes it rained stone, and huge boulders lay where they had dropped from the sky. Dull glows from cracks in the ground told of the immense heat simmering just beneath the crust, which would on occasion bubble up and scour the desert in a flood of fire.

Zeelandis was not merely just dry or hostile, although it was both those things: Zeelandis was malicious. Even when the relentless sun had sunk low in the sky, the heat washed off the endless cracked stone underfoot and leached the very life out of anything that walked there. The land was still hungry, inheriting its hunger from the voracious things that had so suddenly departed. Aside from the lonely carrion birds circling overhead and the lizards that scuttled between patches of shade, there seemed to be no living things here. Certainly a normal human could survive only a few hours on the southern desert of Zeelandis.

The man, whom some called Derkrom, and who was currently quite satisfied to use that name, was not a normal human and had not been one for some time. He felt the desert trying to drag the life out of him through the soles of his feet, but he was made of tougher stuff and refused. He gathered his cloak around him, shielding the back of his head and neck from the glare of the sun burning in the mauve sky. The journey here had been a long one.

In the distance was his objective. Ahead, where the massive chunks of rock had landed here and there, was a formation that might almost have been deliberate. It was lopsided and ugly, like the rest of this place, but the great rock spears jutting from the ground were almost like pillars, the boulders scattered around almost marking out a precinct. Perhaps, seen from the right angle, a long stratified slab of stone was a fallen lintel, and the roughly rectangular chunks were the remains of a fallen wall.

Derkrom understood how such a place, first choked in carnivorous rainforest, then entombed in an equally deadly land of fire and death, could have been missed. The few who had seen this place in the last millennium had no doubt paid little attention to this particular collection of rocks. But Derkrom paid attention to the world around him, and as soon as he saw it there was no doubt in his mind that he had found what he was looking for. It was the lost City of Middelburg and at its center was the great museum complex, which had hosted the Triennials of long ago.

He clambered nimbly over the stones marking the outer boundaries. He was not a young man, but he was still spry. Derkrom glanced around the interior of the collapsed museum. He knew how it had once looked, and was not surprised that it had weakened and fallen, for he also had some idea of what it had been built to contain.

Derkrom then spoke a few words that should never issue from a human throat; he felt their power, and felt his soul squirming against the corruption they held. The ground beneath his feet trembled, not with power but with fear. Fragments of rock tumbled to the ground. Derkrom took a deep breath, remembering how he had used this power long ago for very different ends, and spoke the final syllable.

The ground opened, like pestiferous clockwork. The mechanisms were ancient and the shriek of metal on stone keened from far below as huge sections of the ground pivoted. The stone columns sank like the tumblers of a lock, and immense black metal counterweights swung up from beneath the ground on long armatures. The circular section of the ground on which Derkrom stood shuddered and began to sink, forming a platform fifty meters across that bore Derkrom down into a deep, dark shaft. Arcane machineries whirled massively around him as the platform descended. Cogs spun in the darkness and the rhythmic thunder of titanic clockwork boomed.

After many long minutes, the walls of the shaft above him vanished as the platform passed through a layer of metal and machines into a vast open space. All above was solid black, below hung a landscape of cold metal. As Derkrom sank lower into the chill subterranean world he could make out massive curved walls reaching up and down, for this cavern was a hollow sphere, perhaps ten kilometers in diameter. He was inside the Vleeshal, the ancient and terrible home of the great Triennial.

Derkrom's jaded eyes let him look on it without being dumbstruck, but even he was impressed by the sheer size of the cavity. The circle of stone on which he stood dropped like a mote of light into the darkness, toward the structure the sphere had been built to contain.

A half-glimpsed web of cables suspended a platform in the sphere's center, larger than a city might be in a saner world, fully five kilometers across. Upon this immense suspended plateau was a complex of galleries and exhibition halls, showrooms and studios, built of blue-black metal that glinted strangely in the light filtering down from above. Bridges spanned canyonlike avenues. Pinnacles reached up like blocky metallic fingers toward the open entrance from which he had come, now reduced to a tiny circle of tantalizing light in the surface far above. The buildings reached right to the edge of a platform, maintaining a rigid design that spoke of how the Vleeshal had been created for some greater purpose. At the ancient museum's center was a wide plaza marked out by artificial rivers of quicksilver, with a cluster of galleries on either side stretching to the endless depths of the cavern.

The floating platform on which Derkrom stood finally reached the floor of the silent galleries and dissolved into droplets of mercury, leaving Derkrom on an avenue of polished iron. The metal glowed a faint shimmering blue-gray as the power evaporated off every polished surface. The metal was cold and pale; haloes of condensation formed where his fingers touched it. It was so old it looked new.

Even after all this time, Derkrom was glad to realize he could still be amazed, for this museum-city was amazing, and a testament to the desperation that had once stalked the land. The terror that had forced whole populations to labor on this museum had breached terrible secrets to create its designs, and demanded untold sacrifices in the hope that the Dark Gods would leave it inviolate. They had been truly afraid. Derkrom knew true fear very well – he could taste it here, in the metallic air, and see it in the dull blue shimmer of the buildings.

Down here it was silent, and Derkrom's footsteps echoed as he padded through the galleries. The exhibition complex was made from stacks of steel slabs surrounding rectangular open spaces with faceless monumental forms. All the while, great spotlights loomed overhead. Derkrom could smell the age here, and see the terror in the immense mechanisms swinging through the shadows overhead. The ceiling, perhaps a thousand meters overhead and barely visible in the darkness, was held aloft by an intricate pattern of gothic arches, a pattern so complex as to drive one to madness.

He reached the central plaza, stepping over the geometric channels of quicksilver. The plaza was hundreds of meters across and empty aside from a cluster of buildings in the center, which had once been an enormous gift shop and bistro-cafeteria. The rest of the open space was crisscrossed with miniature artificial rivers of mercury and overlooked by five tall towers that reached, like claws, from the plaza's edge.

Derkrom entered the first building, a vast room with a ceiling so high mist formed in the distant corners. The floor was polished black hardwood and the plaster walls were sculpted into sinuous, suggestive shapes. The pictures hanging on the walls had turned black and dull with only faint, wriggling traces of the living images they had once displayed. Clouds of glowing insects, bound in magical cages hanging from the ceiling, shone a dim, pale light onto the pictures. Derkrom could begin to make out the subject of the pictures in the faint light: trees, dark against the evening sky, great pines and oaks and palms; upon their frames were words written in a strange runic script.

This script had a peculiar straight-lined lettering; a normal man's eyes would bleed from looking at them, for they spelled out the sternest of warnings as well as complex and powerful spell-boundaries. Derkrom knew languages that had never been spoken by human tongues, these ancient runes among them, and he knew how to divert their power around his soul. To utter them, of course, was another matter entirely.

The runes glowed as Derkrom began to speak. His tongue burned and he could feel the skin of his lips splitting in the heat, but he had woven powerful magic before and could withstand the pain. His cloak caught fire and he pulled it over his shoulders, casting it to the ground without missing a syllable. These were dark and dangerous words: they told of power and pain. They had never been written down on paper with ink, because they would come alive and flee from the page. He felt fire in his lungs. The runes were almost too bright to look at now, emitting terrible waves of power as they tried to resist Derkrom's counterspell. The exhibition halls were shuddering. The power trapped for so many centuries within them was threatening to break out. Sounds like thunder from deep within the metal of the floor cracked and rumbled, and quicksilver hissed as it boiled and evaporated.

Derkrom was jolted back, but kept on his feet, denying the force that strove to drive him away from the heart of the Triennial complex. He was yelling now, flames licking from his mouth, his throat raw and burning with every breath. A voice was answering, bellowing from beneath the precinct, a voice that had not been heard for thousands of years.

With a thunderclap, the metal shattered. Derkrom flung a mental shield over himself as white-hot shrapnel exploded all around him, surging in gouts of molten steel near his sphere of protection. He was flung backwards and the buildings flickered by as he hurtled away from the eruption of power. He smashed against a wall at the edge of the central plaza and grabbed on to it, the skin on his fingers soldered to the hot metal, chunks of wreckage coursing past him like a waterfall. The din was so vast he did not hear it at all, his mind blocked it out with a wall of white noise.

When the light died down, Derkrom hauled himself up onto a platform of smoldering metal. His hands and feet were scorched to the bone, but he had suffered such things before. He had felt bullets shear through his body and watched his blood drain away.

The billows of smoke gradually dissipated into the gloom, revealing a huge glowing crater where the central plaza had been. The galleries around it had been blasted to molten slag, the towers reduced to bubbling stumps, the bridges now spindly threads collapsing into the blasted remains. Rivers of black-flecked molten metal oozed toward the crater where the blast had exposed a chamber hidden within the platform. It was like a burst abscess in the metal, where something had been revealed for the first time since fear and desperation had managed to shut it away. The Daemon Curatorum! Known only in legend as "Volf-Sun" the Multus Sanguis itself!

There it stood! Suddenly it began to speak. "Rot flesh and splinter bones! Boil gore, snap spine! The light! All pain to the light!" Its voice was a vast cacophony, like a thousand discordant instruments playing at once. It filled the immense spherical cavity, echoing around the distant metal walls. Even from where he stood, Derkrom's sharp eyes, so much better than a normal man's, cut through the heat haze and could see the creature he had awoken and set free.

"The rage. I remember such rage, like a wall of fire. . . ." the Curatorum breathed massively with the shock of its release, its chest heaving. It was thirty meters tall, the size of a Titan war engine. Gray flesh throbbed with muscles, glistening in the glow of the crater. Its heart was a slab of brass machinery punched through its chest, valves pumping, cogs grinding; driving pistons stabbed from its biceps and thighs, fired by steaming furnaces that gaped from its back. Wings of thick skin stretched between steel frameworks unfolded from its shoulders, and it shook its huge equine head, the fleshy mandibles grinding, the wet red slits of its eyes glowing with anger and joy. "Such desire it was that caged me, such suffering it took. So much hate! Such a river of blood!"

The monster flexed its taloned hands, breathing in the sulfurous air. It gouged one forearm along the jagged, exposed metal of its prison cell and watched the thick, steaming daemon blood flowing across its skin. It held its arm high and let a few drops spatter onto its face, into its eyes, into its mouth, roaring with its lust for violence.

"Blood!" it lamented. "My blood! The pain! It is time!" it bellowed. "Time for the Triennial once again!"

Derkrom stood on the threshold of the crater, and spoke in a sorcerer's voice he knew it could not hear. "Welcome back," he said.

At the bottom of the ocean, flat-bodied scavengers flopped blindly in fear. In the skies, hollow-boned sky-whales circled, dumb with shock. Even the sun-bleached stones and jagged rocks of Zeelandis shuddered when they heard the Daemon's call.

A massive girder plunged down from the suspended ceiling and Derkrom knew that it was time to go. As he exited the cavern he risked looking back and beheld for an instant the terrible creature already at work rebuilding the galleries, soaring on his batlike wings and trailing fire like a meteor. The Daemon Curatorum was laughing, insane with the novelty of his release. "Now I must find the Artists," he roared and his great wings were flapping and he was heading upward and flying off into the sky to begin his search.

Word spread faster than the sun travels across the sky. An event momentous enough will be known in mere hours across the world, as if the seas and winds carried the news. The Triennial was coming and no one was safe! Derkrom hauled himself over the rocks that marked the boundary of ancient Middelburg and ran as fast as he could across the parched ground. The earth shook violently beneath his feet and suddenly lurched, pitching Derkrom onto his face in a depression of the rocky ground, at the bottom of which was a patch of earth. Derkrom crawled down and dug at it with his hands until he touched cold metal. A few words of sorcery carried the soil away to reveal a curved metal surface with blistered paintwork and a small round hatch.

Derkrom passed his hands over the hatch. Sensors beneath the surface bleeped and the locking mechanism clicked open. The hatch swung inward and old air rolled out, carrying a smell of machinery and fuel. A light flickered inside, revealing a single gravity-cushioned seat with a life support hood bolted in front of a bank of controls and displays. Derkrom smiled. It was good to see that his spaceship was still where he had left it.

The control stick unfolded from the central console and Derkrom grasped it, gunning the single large thrust engine. Another firing and the ship was airborne, hurtling up toward the night sky. Derkrom could finally sleep. He had released the Daemon Curatorum and set in motion a chain of events that would change the world forever. He had planned and hoped for this day for a long time: now all that was left was to wait.

Many legends claim to tell of the great Triennials that followed. Triennial legends are among the oldest of the tales told in the courts of the prophets and around the campfires of barbarians, and all the peoples that have ever graced Zeelandis have a different version. There are those who say the Triennial is an egg laid by the gods, which will some day hatch, bringing chaos and madness. Others maintain that it is a gift to the real universe and will act as a bridge across which enlightenment will travel.

But the truth is far simpler.

THE INSTRUCTOR

1. DAWN

5:17 AM

Broadcast: "I felt a hot, enchanting liquid run down my legs, and when she was done, I got up and in turn watered her body, which she complaisantly turned to the unchaste and faintly murmuring spurt on her skin. After thus flooding her cunt, I smeared jizm. . . ."

I reached around to the other side of the bed and turned off the overly assertive voice alarm. The early dawn light filtered in through the dusty venetian blinds and warmly drenched my face. I was sleep deprived and barely conscious. Waking up abruptly after a late night is even more difficult these days because the two suns in our decentered solar system move in nonelliptical orbits. I never know quite how to adjust the blinds the night before so the white sunlight will fall onto the wall above me without hitting my face. Light is such a dark issue in this region of the south plateau. The smaller sun, which is the brightest, occasionally rises during the night, causing disturbances in bio-sleep patterns. The larger sun appears later in another trajectory. It's mind-numbing to keep track of these irregular patterns on a day-to-day basis, and with constant sleep deprivation, being awake is easily confused with dreaming.

While getting out of bed, I trip over a pile of books that teetered on my simulated Eames table. A book entitled *Comedy Is a Man in Trouble* lands on the floor with a thud. I look at it for a moment, then start to think about how one's life is like a comedy, and then drift on to wondering what the relationship might be between slapstick and Deconstruction. I seem to lose track of time for a moment. Also on the table are two small, black plastic battery-powered clocks that I acquired through an underground Time auction. Between the two clocks I am able to average the approximate time, as no one in our region is allowed access to the real time. It's not available due to the recent simultaneity, and basically everyone depends on bio-calendars anyway. One of the clocks has an outdated radio frequency feature which I rigged to use as an alarm. I need the alarm just in case neither sun appears, which they have been known to do since the last offsite superimposition. The presets on the clock alarm are no longer legible, so I happened to select the all-day and all-night spoken-word and porn frequency. That frequency is still being transmitted – or more likely is just collecting and polluting the cellular frequency mass. These are the forgotten transgressive programs made for radio plays and readings that have celebrities and other actors performing or reading sex. This morning's selection was from Mr G. Bataille.

Time is a nostalgic artifact of the past that I just like to keep around. The white sunlight bleaches everything in the atmosphere, including those invisible specks of dust that mindlessly sparkle, floating gravity-free, around my head. I feel them hit the surface of my skin as if they are magnetized. I can hear them collide as I get out from under the sheets, stand on the bare floor, and stretch up toward the ceiling. I walk over the creaky surface to the dirty, tinted window and reach up and separate two of the blinds so I can get a clear view through the massive window to see what the morning looks like; dust flies from the blind. As I peer out, I'm relieved to see the mauve-tinted sky with the burnt red sun just above the watery horizon. I miss being able to regularly count on that and I'm sure everyone would agree. Ultimately, the days of sameness and predictability were so reassuring. Not too long ago, there was only one sun and a consistent moon. It's hard to accept, but I know those times are gone forever. I remember how things used to be and I try to get through the day with a kind of self-prescribed optimism, usually with an acoustic injection.

From the window the trees, lush foliage, and other domestic ports are poetically silhouetted against the colorful morning sky which by now has shuttle streams crisscrossing as far as you can see. The continuous trails will be suspended all day, doubling as clouds and reminding us of a previous and forgotten skyscape. The trails blur together with the cables, poles, signs, and wires that support the never-ending conglomeration of networks which surround all of us all the time, like water streaming from a fountain. The fragments of a post-communication culture collapse into the constructed props and images of nature. The flattened perception of the outside might as well be a shiny, varnished oil painting on a stiff wooden panel. One could almost construe this suffocating and airless spectacle as romantic.

As I stand at the window I see Mobile Ground Pods. The MGPs are beginning to back up on the ETS (External Transport Surface) in long and fast-moving strings of humming harmonies. I shower and get dressed, knowing I soon have to leave the comforts of my domestic port and travel to my repeated and daily mission, CAD (Center for Art and Design), like many other players on this plateau. My partner Conal calls down from the platform above, "Do you want breakfast?"

I hear Lane in the background screaming, "No, no, no, Daddy."

I respond in my tired state, "Yeah, be right up." I look forward to the scone and black coffee that will help get me out the door. But there is a lot between now and then that I must take care of.

2. DEPARTURE

7:27 AM

Conal and Lane embrace me with warm hugs and good-byes as I exit the small, dark transition chamber of our grayish, low-ceilinged port. Lane is only two-and-a-half and doesn't yet realize that I am fully committed to my role of Culture Service Provider and Institutional Game Player – though he does spend a lot of time working with language drawings on his computer. Once outside the port, I immediately see that the atmosphere is bright and abrasive, so blurry and dense that I use protection: special lenses, surface ointments, and appropriate clothing. I do detect a subtle hint of a mid-westerly layer, but perhaps just for the morning. Mid-westerly layers tend to move in at dawn and for a few moments they shade and filter the blinding daylight atmosphere of the outside.

They usually pass over quickly, especially during this part of the season when there are excessive routing patterns. A mid-westerly may – on occasion and unannounced – induce an intense psychological moment, uncomfortably introspective, in some players. The somewhat soothing effects allow one's body to gently relax and progress forward on autoped. I soon gather my thoughts and take notice of what is going on around me as I walk over to the MGP bay. Numerous polygonal birds perched in the gilded tree soon expand my experience. Modular hexagonal redwood decking is under my feet. I inspect the garden for deterrents. Entering the slanted bay I move around the various piles of unwanted (and hopefully, soon to be discarded) commodities from which we are never quite free. The bay for us and for many, I think, functions as a holding station for old and unwanted commodities, until the rovers are given access to them. After opening the gate and securing it, I enter my vehicle and fire the ignition. When I hear all the lifters in sequence, I engage drive and accelerate onto the approach pad. The gate is secured and I'm ready for departure. Today I will be going to one of the adjacent societies where there is a CAD; it is a cover for something that I cannot describe now. CADs are institutions, like everything else; Conal is funded by one too. We both spend a lot of time there each week conducting private research and discussing seemingly forward-thinking ideas with colleagues and students.

3. EN ROUTE

7:52 AM

The MGP that I currently use is an older model that was

originally imported, but had been carefully maintained by its previous user. It expresses its rather outdated mechanical qualities rather simply and directly, which appeals to me. I'm sure its firing is a disturbance to the neighboring ports and bays, but no one has complained, nor have I been fined by the Sector for emissions. It also seems to possess some personal mnemonic attributes, which I cannot seem to separate myself from. This model has a mid-engine drive train with two storage bays; it sits low and hovers wonderfully over the ground plane at zero gravity. The one problem is that it's difficult for some of the MGP operators to see me, as many are massive and tower above me. My MGP barely comes up to their impact plates. And with dark-tinted windscreens, it's not easy to see who is behind those massive, unwieldy chambers. As with many technologies, MGPs are extensions of the body, not only aiding task performance, but also functioning as an outward expression of internal psychological streams: paranoia, aggression, and power – like surrogates of one's personality.

My mind starts to drift as I'm thinking about Conal and Lane . . . while hearing the sounds from the whining gearbox. Operating this MGP over the undulating surfaces and navigating between other, larger MGPs is relaxing. I will be arriving at CAD very soon. The route doesn't take that long and it's a combination of both high-speed and slower ETS's. I'm traveling quite fast now and the whitish haze from the atmosphere is sticking to my windscreen. The sounds of the wind and the other outside forces moving across the windscreen combine with all the other automatic noises into a mechanical, symphonic cacophony. The slower route is flanked by the lush foliage that I mentioned earlier, and now I am immersed in it. I arrive at the beginning of the winding ETS and select a Kenny G file for the playback system. As I fumble with the controls I suddenly hear from the receiver, "Full of muck, she climaxed in a liberating frenzy. She deeply inhaled our pungent and happy odor. 'You smell like Marcel,' she buoyantly confided after a hefty climax, her nose under my wet ass."

Kenny G is a necessary foreground acoustic action for preparing one's entry into CAD; the smooth continuous wave-tones enter into my subconscious like a narcotic, clearing out interference and lifting me up. I hit shuffle and repeat. Someone once told me that Kenny G held the record for holding a note the longest, though I never understood what that was supposed to mean. The gravitational forces increase as the pod moves quickly back and forth, following the surface and turns of the prescribed route. Kenny G seems to mimic and align with the motion; the whole traveling experience is virtually and psychedelically cinematic.

4. THE INSTITUTE

7:56 AM

The final approach is just ahead. I engage the throttle while still buzzing on Kenny G and accelerate ahead, winding around into the entrance of CAD. I must now focus on the day ahead. As I dock my vintage pod into the faculty bay, I'm going over what has to be presented and recalling the projects we were intensely discussing and working on last week. I recall something about containers and interface, and the experience-as-site. Hopefully I will be more on top of things once I'm inside the CAD port where the air is very cold and filtered. I wave my data across the scanner and I am in the north wing where we all hang out and do research. I enter and see the lab is open, but first I head to the lounge to contact Janson about what we were working on last week. Good, I have the room to myself with the exception of the surveillance cameras and code-only entry. I am always being watched and recorded; we cannot escape that anywhere we go. I reach Janson, my colleague and co-teacher, on the micro-cellular. He's in his office port and as usual, he's buried with rapid prototypes, databooks, computers, and samples of software from sales demos.

Dane: "Janson."

Janson: "Yes, Dane, how are you?"

Dane: "Okay, thanks. What do you have for today?"

Janson: "Yeah, I've got some new images to present and talk about. By the way, which text did you want to discuss?"

Dane: "Let's go for a follow-up with the discussion on that idea of container-as-interface, I liked that a lot, it's one of those ideas that has really stuck with me. . . ."

Janson: "There is so much more to say on that subject. I think we could bring in anything we want to, don't you think? 'Mass Customization'?"

Dane: "Yes, I do, but I don't want to neglect the importance of anticipation and experience as site-in-itself, you know? 'It's not the object itself, but the anticipation and experience or interface itself as site.' 'So, we are literally saying that context defers meaning.'"

Janson: "You could say that, but we already know the relationship of context to meaning. 'Let's focus on the nonphysical now.'"

Dane: "Context-as-container, it shapes the interface between the subject and object."

Janson: "I have to go now, there's a blockage."

Dane: "Okay, see you in class very soon. Bye."

I disengage, but so many other related ideas are swirling around in my head. I drift for a while and remember that Conal refers to these moments I have as "dog moments." Our world is mass-customized and I want to discuss how it has evolved, going all the way back to Nike and Pepsi. I have just enough time to assemble a coffee from upstairs and get to class. The students are usually a little late anyway and my teaching assistant, Mikella, will get the readings together. The CAD nourishment bar is above average (as far as institutions go), and is a supreme example of how mass-customization functions in the food service industry. Of course the Starbacks Corporation has the coffee service; they also sponsor a lifestyle studio at CAD. CAD is like a big motherboard and all the sponsored sections are self-contained plug-ins. I select my coffee ingredients and head downstairs to our room with my nonfat-soy iced double espresso latte. The white-walled and concrete-floored classroom is a large, slightly less finished space with a few smaller alcoves and galleries for temporary experiments and installations. There are no windows and it is always very cold. There are remnants of projects and materials everywhere: foams, waxes, metals, postconsumer products, and a few images spanning the walls.

We use the grounds and other spaces too, for other site-related projects that might be more physically connected to the Modernist site. The classroom also tends to be a place where pieces of discarded lobby furniture such as sofas and overstuffed chairs end up. This gives the space a kind of raw domestic ambience, in contrast to the rest of the center, which holds to more outdated and conformist standards. Like many other ports on the south plateau, the CAD port is situated in a fictionalized landscape of various thematic plant life-forms. There is an earnest effort in Behavioral Development to cater to the staged authenticity and the memory of the real. Synthetic watering systems generate the appearance of actual maintenance and the entire compound has a feeling of being in an illustration or simulation. The smell of grass and foliage is aromatherapy-enhanced for a completely mood-elevated and controlled environmental experience. One class is going through all the motions of designing and building a garden on campus. They are performing the physical acts of designing and gardening as a way to try to understand the loss of past origins. The rectangular CAD port with its shiny black beams and concrete grids recalls an old style of late Modernism: the honesty and expression of intent is allegedly inscribed into the building itself, with pipes, ducts, and other systems all exposed. The CAD site is also a tourist stop for many visiting the south plateau and it is not uncommon to see groups of tourists peering into designated classrooms, hoping to get a glimpse of what this kind of education might look like. There are classrooms specifically designed like a stage, with front room and back room, and large picture windows on both sides so tourists may look in at any time to see "behind the scenes." The students and instructors who occupy those spaces are more or less acting.

5. CLASS

8:16 AM

Sounds emanate from the surrounding high speed ETS, generating a low, echoing, white noise that reverberates within the hallways and air passages. I find this very calming and I am ready to begin the class. Students are hanging around the doorway, others are waiting in the back room, papers are being shuffled, books and samples of materials are being passed around. Janson comes in right after me and we talk for a minute before I ask if anyone has any announcements that might be of interest to the rest of the class. Everyone looks around and a few comments are made and we move on to discuss the students' work. Besides the ongoing discussions regarding the previous definitions and new practices of site-specificity, we have also been talking about the future interfaces between types of practices, commodities, contexts, and artworks. One student, Robbi, had set up a situation in one of the gallery spaces, so we all follow her over there.

Once inside the mostly white room we immediately see that the structural components of the space are brought to our attention by an application of the color red; one small angled wall near the door is now a creamy beige. There are two large mirrored plastic silhouettes of Modernist furniture on the opposite wall, and in one corner, low to the ground, is a grouping of laser-cut and etched mirrored waveforms. In the opposite corner a data monitor sits on a small authentic Eames table. The video is of the vertical red beam in the space with intercut images of young males in underwear looking at it through a peephole. A slightly hopeful potted plant sits close to the actual beam. The sounds of water and wind are also audible on the soundtrack. We walk around the installation and then sit down. I start the discussion with a question about the depiction of males in the video and the relationship to the vintage Modernist space we are sitting in. Robbi starts talking about her intentions and the various citations that have been superimposed within the project. She goes on about outmoded issues pertaining to composition and the comparison between Modernist ideas, spiritual utopias, and Feng Shui.

She explains, "I want my work to promote living life to its fullest potential, in a balanced and harmonious manner, through an understanding of our relationship to our living and working environments. Everything is energetically connected and always changing: your consciousness is represented in your environment."

As the class begins to understand what she means we go off on many digressions and tangents about Modernism and Feng Shui, and how behavior and atmospheres are physically generated and programmed. It seems that Robbi's project is attempting to correct what she has determined to be a defect, a deficit of the space, or a restoration of a certain feeling about the space. Janson forms a question regarding the revival of Logocentricism and the relationship to metaphysics.

Robbi responds, "This project is about the understanding of the physical aspects of our environments, as well as the invisible aspects of our environments, as they relate to direction, time, and space – as did Modernism."

Another student in the class asks her about what she meant by *properly aligned in our environments.*

"These environments enable each of us to live richer, fuller, happier lives; we are more enabled to actualize our full potential in life," Robbi says. "When good Modernism is in place it supports our health, wealth, and relationships."

Janson eagerly responds to Robbi, "Space in the abstract is the formless constituent of architecture that is formed in architectural or urban design and contained or defined by the bounding planes – the walls, floors, ceilings – into space, in the immediate, which is the specific character of the 3D aspect of the building or buildings. When space acquires use, habit, and history, it becomes place."

I ask Robbi about her thoughts regarding the sexuality of the project and the displacement of the male gaze. We find ourselves talking more about the atmosphere itself and other various anxieties related to either Modernism or Feng Shui before we have to stop and return to the classroom.

After the break, Janson and I present our material to the class regarding mass-customization and its relationship to the practice and discourse of art production. The rest of the time goes by very fast; we are all surprised to come to the end of the class so soon. Janson and I head upstairs to have lunch and sit outside in the Butterfly Pavilion.

6. HOME

3:45 PM

We join a few other instructors in the Pavilion, your usual hyperreal sense-heightened enclosure where the intense white light is monitored to orchestrate the mood and motion patterns of the occupants while they eat. The recently expanded CAD campus is a virtual theme park of what education should look like from a tourist's point of view. But, as we all know, any institution represents an imbalance of power and is loaded with human flaws and inadequacies. Nearing the atrium, I stop off at the central library to pick up material for tomorrow's class; by this time of the day I am tired and ready to head back to the domestic port to re-energize. As I walk the rest of the way down the long sparkling glass hallway to the north faculty bay I see a few former students whose names I can't seem to recall. I just say hello and then remember that I was supposed to send out a file for Robbi. Her project needs to go to a destination space in another atmosphere for an upcoming exhibition. All of her work is post-digital so it's not a problem for it to be transmitted at the last minute. The faculty port is just ahead. I enter through the shiny black door and find an available file transferring station, load the file, set the code, and it is sent instantly. I am relieved to have remembered to do that, as many times details like that fall through the cracks. In the hallway again, I spot the exit and prepare to move outside and into the whitish-mauve hazy humid atmosphere of the south plateau. A blast of hot sticky air washes over me as I slowly walk through the exit gates. I quickly pull on my jacket, put on dark lenses and a hat, and walk quickly to my MGP. The light is odd and omnidirectional as the second sun is barely starting to appear at the horizon line, which is directly in my view all the way home.

THE DRONE

1.

Space-Time Travel Disorientation. STTD. Some say it's the jet lag of the twenty-second century. But it's nothing like normal time-zone jet lag. If you think time-zone jet lag is bad, well, STTD really fucks you over. What fucks you over – and fucks you over in a brutal way – is what they call the space-time travel paradox. This paradox says that the time you spend traveling is way longer than the time it takes to get to your destination. So technically, you age more when you travel than when you stay put. Nobody really understands how this works, except physicists. And I think even they don't really understand it. Technically maybe, but I'm never convinced they can actually wrap their brains around the *concept* of the space-time travel paradox. No one can. That's one of the reasons why they invented the term STTD. It distracts you from pondering the paradox. The other reason is that STTD sounds friendlier. Like being dizzy, or something. But it's not, it's a nightmare.

In our time, traveling is not for the rich – the rich stay home. It's the poor and desperate who do the traveling. Once traveling was a luxury, like pale skin was a luxury in the nineteenth century, pale skin being the sign you were rich enough not to have to work in the sun, out in the fields. In the twentieth century, the fashion in skin color changed from pale to tanned – tanned being the color of those who were rich enough to go on holiday and travel at their leisure. Traveling was a luxury, until space-time travel was invented. When that started happening, the rich made sure they stayed put. They didn't like the aging part, of course, but more importantly the space-time travel paradox drives some people insane. Literally. If not, chances are the sheer boredom of being in a space-time travel pod for months on end will drive you insane.

There are rich people who space-time travel. Kids, usually – boys. Because they want to see something of the universe, they say, and because they're bored. Even more bored than the boredom that comes with traveling, or so they *think*. Everybody knows why they really do it – even their fathers, who have often done it themselves (but won't admit it), and try to stop them. Two reasons: first, they go because of the romantic appeal of boredom. Mistake. Second, because of what they think lies at the end of their odyssey, what we, space-time travelers, the poor, do to counter STTD: sex, drugs, and transgressive behavior. Wrong again. Well, there is sex, drugs, and transgressive behavior, yes. But it's nothing like their fantasies.

2.

I enter the underground concrete and Kevlar bunker, and I'm about two-and-a-half hours early. It happens all the time, when you're suffering from STTD. You come late or early, but never on time, because you always get it wrong.

Normally, in a place like this, it doesn't matter when you come. It's always the same here. It's supposed to be like this. It's a place where people with severe STTD like to come, because there seems to be no time here, only the present. People come here for what is called the Drone. The Drone is a very, very loud noise. It sounds big and industrial, somewhat like the sound of the engines of a space-time travel pod. Only louder, much louder. Much of the sound you experience physically, through your body. The Drone makes your whole body resonate, giving you a sense of presence. The sound itself is very repetitive. It takes a while to get into it. At first it's just too loud. But once you get into it, it can be very liberating. And after spending seventy-eight days in a pod, as I just did, you need a little liberation.

You won't find the Drone on Earth. That's because the Drone is not for the rich. It's a poor man's thing. The rich don't need it. They don't travel, remember? Out here, halfway across the universe, there is nothing to remind you of the better world the rich have created for themselves. When you exit a Drone bunker, as places like these are called, you enter an ugly and lonely world. And that's exactly what you want, after months of traveling. You don't want the beauty of luxury. You don't want the aesthetics of control. You don't want things to be organized, or taken care of: you want darkness, despair, disarray. That, or to get fucked, cry, and be comforted afterward. And then to sleep. And to be left alone after that. If all that's not immediately available, you go for the Drone.

It's always packed here, in the Drone bunker. Fifteen hundred bodies, I estimate. Only a few rich kids, trying to blend in, but standing out. Everybody here is sweating. When I walk around, I not only see and feel people, I smell people. It's even busier than normal. I'm probably not the only one who has come here with an ulterior motive. And I'm probably not the only one here to investigate the rumor that something in the Drone has changed.

After what seems a very long time a new Drone Driver shows up at the controls. He's the rumored genius people have told me about, the Drone prodigy. When he started showing up a couple of months ago, the rumor that he was changing the Drone started spreading fast. Tonight, the change he initiates in the Drone comes subtly, it's hardly noticeable. At first I question myself, as if I hadn't been paying attention and had missed a beat. But then I notice the whole atmosphere in the Drone bunker is changing. Fifteen hundred sweaty bodies stir, become alert, and react to the change in the Drone. The steady rhythm of the Drone shifts suddenly, again and again, and every time it does, the crowd goes wild. Still, the changes are hardly noticeable. But somewhere in the sonic layers of the Drone, something incredibly *musical* is developing. We all notice it – we are all *here* now.

The Drone was always reassuringly familiar: colossal, monotone, and brainless. But now, it seems that behind the Drone there is an intelligent plan. Everything you look for in the Drone is still there. It's still very loud and very physical. It's still comforting. It still gives you a sense of time and place. But the stupidity and senselessness have gone. There is beauty now. Not an abstract beauty, like logarithms. Not an artificial beauty, like the world the rich create for themselves. Not the beauty of universal truths people keep going on about. But a beauty that comes out of dread and ugliness. A beauty found in reality.

There's a girl standing in front of me, moving slowly in time with the Drone. Black hair, blue eyes, creamy pale skin, glistening with sweat. She's clearly on a Drone Rider, a pill that's both very popular and very illegal. It enhances your senses, opens you up to the Drone, and makes you very, very horny. I took them myself for a while. Until the time I woke up under sheets covered in blood and strands of long red hair (not mine). I didn't discover any open wounds on my body, only lots of bruises, and my dick was swollen and painful. The girl I had been with that night, both of us on Drone Riders, was gone without a trace. I never saw her again, and the memory of what happened never came back completely; I remember some of the sex, but have no idea where all the hair and blood came from. For a while after, I watched the news anxiously, but the crime reports never mentioned a redhead.

Her back toward me, the girl with the black hair and blue eyes takes my hand. Her sweaty palm is fondling, almost chewing mine. She moves closer. Our hands are pressed between my crotch and her round ass. She keeps moving her ass, slowly grinding our hands between us. She feels me getting hard. It's nice for a while, but I lose interest. Normally I wouldn't. No way. But now I want to concentrate on the changes in the Drone. The changes take me to what seems like a collective consciousness. After a while, the girl turns round and looks at me, surprised. She points to my nose. The Drone has given me a nosebleed. With every thud of the Drone, a small spray of blood is knocked out from inside my head, onto my shirt, and onto the floor. I gesture to her that I don't care. All I want is to be inside the change in the Drone.

3.

A long time later – hours? A day? – I stand outside, empty and indecisive. The prodigy Drone Driver has been replaced. He'll be back in a few days. The Drone is back to normal. I feel a little better, my STTD seems to have worn off a bit. Two rich kids walk by, scared, looking at my shirt. They look disappointed too. Probably couldn't get their hands on a Drone Rider, or on a girl who took one. And the STTD, they thought they could handle it, but they seem to be in very bad shape. I decide to go back to my hotel alone. The girl with the black hair and blue eyes had lost interest in me a while after I had lost interest in her. Later, I saw her kissing some guy. I don't remember her leaving.

In my hotel room, the fluorescent light in the bathroom is broken. It won't go on or off, just staying somewhere in between. It zooms irregularly, trying to switch on, sounding like a bug flying into something all the time. You never really wake up, or sleep, after space-time travel. If you're lucky you nod and drool a little. When you regain some consciousness after such a nod-and-drool episode, you're disoriented in both space and time. *Where* am I? *When* am I?

And then there is the eternal third question: *what* am I doing here? Well, I was sent by the very powerful and nameless consortium that owns Middelburg – a beach resort for the elderly rich, somewhere along the north European coast. Life there is very quiet and completely free of crime. Of course, they learned long ago that we couldn't live without fear. There has to be some element of danger in our lives, otherwise we physically and mentally shut down. We become numb. This is only a problem for the rich, of course. The poor have enough to worry about. So anyway, the consortium that owns Middelburg is big on what they call "danger management." "In Middelburg, we allow just enough carefully controlled danger in your life to keep you enjoying the luxury of safety!"

The nameless consortium has tried lots of stuff before. I guess you also have to be innovative in "danger management." You need an element of surprise. Now they want to organize the first Middelburg Art Triennial. And that's why I'm here. They want the prodigy Drone Driver at their Triennial and I'm supposed to take care of it. I guess it's like what I've been told: the rich who founded the town were collecting the strange from afar, to study it in the safety of their own environment. Exoticism, really. I don't know if it worked then, but it won't work now. You'll never be inside the Drone in a beach resort for the elderly. It just wouldn't be the same thing without STTD, without the despair, the loneliness. It would never work in a perfect world.

After deciding that, for the moment, I don't care if I will succeed in my mission, I finally drift off. My mind ends up locked between the sound of the stuttering fluorescent in the bathroom and a ringing in my ears. I try to discover something of the Drone in this mix, but don't. In three months, I'll travel back. I will arrive after fourteen days, but will be stuck in a pod for 104.

SHAPESHIFTER

Like a dead straight scar across the Florida landscape, the multiple rails of a giant launching track at its end – surrounded by vehicles and gantries – an enormous glass spaceplane lay waiting in a pool of light. "I can't believe that I, Gina Ashcraft, have sunk this low. Only complete losers do group shows off-world!" I mumbled to myself as my taxi rolled up to the departure loading area of the spaceport. At least I had the right outfit; I was wearing a vintage silver-colored Rudi Gernreich jumpsuit from the 1960s that was so tight that I couldn't really zip up the front, causing my full, perfectly shaped breasts to explode out the top. It was also way too tight in the ass and I could sense that all the weird creatures that were in line with me at check-in were staring at the folds of my clit, which were readily visible. I was just about at the front of the line when I spotted it. A creature – or should I say a blob? – of iridescent Vaseline-colored jelly was pushing, or sliding, its Halliburton luggage onto the scale. "Unbelievable!" I said out loud. "Isn't that thing going to ruin the upholstery of the spaceplane?"

"They have special plastic seat liners," said the spaceport attendant as she waved me forward to a free spot at the ticket counter.

Since about the year 2070 the space agency has been trying to bring a little culture to the space stations, which means they convert half a cargo bay into exhibition space and then hire a curator to put together a group show on the cheap. Usually aliens, but always one or two artists from Earth just to validate the whole thing. "It's worth it, I guess, to see outer space once in your lifetime, feel weightlessness, all that stuff," I was telling myself as I took my seat by the third row window in the tiny spacecabin. The trim stewardess walked by offering moist towelettes and squeeze-bottles of orange juice.

"Takeoff's in five minutes," she said, giving me a slightly embarrassed but charming smile.

The pilot's voice was firm and confident as it came over the cabin speaker. "Please observe all zero-G regulations. We will be docking at Space Station Twenty in about forty-five minutes."

The ship was completely made of the new glass, lighter than a feather and stronger than the hardest steel. It was hardly necessary to sit next to a window for you could see right through the walls, full of conduits and pipes also made of glass and carrying different brightly-colored liquids. Attached to the inner walls and running the length of the spaceship was an especially large conduit with a gold-colored substance running inside it: I thought that it must be the rocket fuel. At the level of my head was a smaller conduit with a blue Tidy-Bowl coloring that emerged from the lavatory (the only part of the ship still made of opaque traditional materials) just at the head of the cabin. "I hope I won't have to see any turds float by," I was saying to myself when out of the corner of my eye I spotted Mr Vaseline sliding up the aisle. I quickly shoved my red-and-white vintage TWA flight bag into the empty seat next to me in the hope of making it look occupied and then turned my head to the window, pretending to look at the landscape but really praying with all my heart that the creature would pass by my row. I was out of luck. I turned my head a few seconds later to find the stewardess had removed my bag and was applying a fitted plastic sheet to the seat adjoining mine. "She must have known, the bitch!" I said to myself as the yellow gelatinous mound eased into the seat next to mine and the stewardess attached his safety harness.

I couldn't help but stare, and after a few seconds I realized that this creature was far from merely an undistinguished mass of jelly. I began to see a distinct headlike shape, with what seemed to be orifices – mouth, eyes, even a nose or two. And below, a pointed protuberance shaped a bit like the top of a meringue. Then to my complete surprise it began to speak. "Hey, baby, you're hot!"

The voice seemed to come from the slight indentation at the center of its uppermost bulge. At the very same moment I noticed that the meringue was beginning to grow, shaping itself into a tubular protrusion and almost doubling in length. "You can squeeze it if you like," it said, as the protrusion swelled again in size, this time reaching almost the height of the tray table and beginning to swerve in my direction.

"Listen, Floyd," I yelled, loud enough so that everyone in the cabin could hear, "keep your JELL-O to yourself!"

Just at this moment the rockets at the rear of the ship started to roar; the countdown had begun. I quickly attached my seat harness, which buckled around my hips and under my crotch, and I noticed the meringue erection had completely dissipated next to me. I attached my headset and turned the channel to space hits, then settled back into a comfortable position and looked out the window. Just as the rockets started to blast, forcing me back into my seat, my favorite song started to play. The G-forces felt good against my body and I felt like the full awesome power of the rockets was burrowing into me. I couldn't move my head or arms and my eyelids and lips slid back under the pressure. I could just see the stars becoming visible through the haze; we were shooting through veils of crimson and pink and gold and blue, finally ending in the blackness of space, and I began to sing along with the music. "If you're listening Mr UFO Man / Speak to Jesus tell him we're on earth and / Things are worse then they have ever been now / Father, it's urgent, we need you, come down." I had almost lost sense of space and time when the pressure and noise abruptly slackened, and the cabin speaker announced, "Preparing to separate from lower stage." There was a slight jolt; the thunder of the engines dropped to a distant roar, then a gentle hiss. The stewardess came walking up the narrow corridor of the closely-spaced seats. There was a slight buoyancy to her steps, and her feet came away from the floor reluctantly as if entangled in glue. She was keeping to the bright yellow band of Velcro carpeting that ran the full length of the floor – and the ceiling. The carpet and the soles of her go-go-boots were covered with myriads of tiny hooks, so that they clung together like burrs. We were in zero gravity!

"In-flight magazine anyone?" she said and handed one to me.

To my horror, on the cover of the magazine under the headline "Young Artists from Outer Space" was a picture of the very same blob that was sitting to my right. "He must be part of the same group show as me," I said to myself, and then I remembered the shapeshifter artists from some planet in the Alpha Centaurus complex that could transform themselves into their own work. "Extraterrestrial Conceptualism" was the new thing and the curators loved it, mainly because there were no shipping costs, hotel rooms, or dinners. These guys would show up, shapeshift into their own work, and then sit there for the duration of the exhibition. They couldn't even come to the opening! The oversized gummi bear from hell in the seat next to mine was named Feng and he was known for changing himself into ordinary household furniture: chairs, tables, etc. He had been in every intergalactic biennial for the last few years and was already a celebrity.

I was pressing my face against the walls of the spaceship, admiring the lights of the stars glistening in the multicolored conduits of glass, musing to myself all the while about the irony of life, when I felt something slimy inserting itself into the gap between my jumpsuit and the cleavage of my ample pointy breasts. Instinctively I jabbed my elbow back, pinning the slippery greenish tentacle, and with my knee I violently pushed up on the armrest, crushing it between the seats. I heard a doleful whimper as my neighbor's whole body seemed to deflate to half its former size. When the serpentine appendage had been absorbed back into his body, Feng slipped out of the seat and down the aisle toward the back of the plane. "Good riddance!" I thought, and tried to wipe off the mayonnaise-like residue it had left on my clothes and skin with a moist towelette. It wasn't doing the job so I decided to go to the restroom and get some proper paper towels.

I put on the Velcro slippers hiding inside the seat pocket in front of me, and started slowly up the aisle toward the bathroom. I tried to walk as gracefully as possible, but ended up almost losing my foothold on the carpet and floating in the air. Someone once said that you could be terrified in space, but that you could not be worried there. Obviously that person had never been in a hurry to get to the wc to clean off the slime of an alien pervert. Upon reaching the bathroom, I pulled the door shut and locked the latch. I found myself in a little cubicle with all the fittings of an ordinary airline toilet, but illuminated with a red light that was very harsh and unpleasant to the eye. A notice printed in prominent letters announced, MOST IMPORTANT! FOR YOUR OWN COMFORT PLEASE READ THESE INSTRUCTIONS CAREFULLY! I sat down on the seat – one still tended to do so even when weightless – and started to unzip my jumpsuit. I admired in the tiny mirror the perfect plum-shaped mounds of my nipples as they protruded from my Kevlar-yellow bra. To get my legs out of the jumpsuit in that tiny cramped space I had to perform spectacular acrobatic maneuvers, placing one leg behind my back and the other over my head. My clear vinyl Barbarella-style panties had gotten caught on the doorknob and had been pulled down halfway to my knees, exposing the perfect elliptical mound of my cunt. I was stuck! For a moment it seemed funny. I could see the headline: "Gina Ashcraft Found Stuck in Spaceship Lavatory." Too bad Jerry Lewis wasn't on board!

I struggled to free myself, to no avail, when all of a sudden the box on the wall containing the paper toilet seat covers began to melt like a clock in a Salvador Dali painting. It quickly morphed until it had acquired the shape and substance of an enormous translucent yellow-green dildo.

"Feng!" I grunted as the head of the dildo, which was actually quite pleasing to look at, forced its way onto my clit and started a slow but steady movement upward. The slippery jellylike substance slid easily into me and I couldn't help but scream with pleasure. I guess I must have been screaming pretty loudly because the stewardess started to bang on the door of the cubicle and I could hear the voices of angry passengers urging her to use her passkey. The huge green dildo started to melt away and to my amazement changed itself into an exact replica of a bar of soap, complete with spaceplane logo. My panties had somehow dislodged themselves from the doorknob and I was able to pull my jumpsuit up over my ass.

"I'm coming out, don't worry," I yelled.

I started to open the bathroom door, but then – as if without thinking – I reached down and picked up the bar of soap and plunged it into the toilet, quickly depressing the flush lever. *Woooosshhh thuddd* went the apparatus as I closed the door of the bathroom on my way back to my seat. I arrived at my seat just in time to see the tiny bar of soap carried past inside the Tidy-Bowl blue conduit. I could swear I saw a tiny face on the soap, which seemed to be saying in a very distant and tiny voice, "Help me! Help me!"

The curator welcomed me warmly in the arrival lounge at Space Station Twenty. He was bubbling about his great idea to put my work in the same room in the exhibition as Feng, the hot new artist from Alpha Centaurus. But where was Feng? We waited and waited and the curator started to get worried and a bit angry. Then I had a wonderful idea! When the curator wasn't looking I walked over to the space station bistro pub and grabbed one of the chairs. It was also made of the new glass and its curving elements were perfectly transparent. I presented it to the curator, who immediately grabbed it with a huge smile and declared, "Feng! You are such a genius! Thonet! Brilliant! Brilliant!"

"GACK V" VARIOUS VENUES

BY SINICO LEAR ART UNIVERSE'S INTERGALACTIC CORRESPONDENT

Despite financial difficulties resulting from the liquidation of the Colacort Corp, its primary sponsor, the fifth Gack triennial, "Gack V," took place this past Brumaire amid widespread pageantry. The triennial was held in several structures in and around Gack, on the seventh planet in the Sirius chain: at the Asimoff – a garish, restless hotel in CenterCity, in a giant Kreuzfeld Apparatus on the outskirts of the megalopolis, and on two orbiting astral sockets by the celebrity Uranusian architect Daniel Lovechild.

According to its curators, the Bollingbroke twins, the exhibition was intended to foster "the interrogation of current contexts of artistic production and reception." These contexts doubtlessly included the seminal influences of solar systemization and new massmediauras, the destruction of thanatic predispositions, and the rapid proliferation of spectralpods. Drawing on the fashionable theories of Vlad Impala-Zembla, whose "Flutterby" opened up new arenas in which to consider these intertwined phenomena, the Bollingbrokes (rather vaguely, it must be admitted) argued for "an expansion of the locus of the disciplinary models that constitute and define the project's intellectual and cultural interest," and, in so doing, expose "a range of social, political, and cultural networks that have marked the limit of solar system discourse today."

Unlike other recent triennials – Alpha Centauri's "Alphafest," Rimron's "Felicit Emptor," and Xantar City's "Collectors Collect Collectibles," each of which featured frenzied bidding wars by institutional and interplanetary investors – "Gack V" sought to avoid the pervasive snares of the intergalactic marketplace by casting a glance at artistic production in the past three centuries, with art made back in the days of universalization, and, before that, spheralization, and even globalization on Earth and elsewhere. There was, consequently, a rather quaint reliance on human producers which, given the blighted current crop of young 'bot artists, proved a fruitful gambit.

Among the 1,776 works by the 365 artists/collectives, many of which had to be viewed with powerful microscopes, or, conversely, from land orbiters, a few must be singled out. Craphonso Phutatorius, from Fofurraville (Quim IV), presented "Lumps," three lumps of molded clay that sat on a little platform in a corner of the Asimoff. The clay was coated in thick roseate glaze and studded with multicolored feathers and sequins that seemed to have been attached with tiny brass cup hooks. With its extreme simplicity and chthonic gravity, "Lumps" harked back to one of those mid-twenty-second-century neo-tribalist works that so enthralled the art world before being displaced by the famed "return of the weal" at the end of that woeful century.

Elsewhere in the Asimoff was a huge transparent aquarium containing digitized imitations of all forms of underwater life. Suspended within a light blue liquid were projections of extraordinary dappled colors flitting about, in the mode that recalled the legends of sea creatures on Earth before the WMD crisis of the twenty-first century. The Katya Wilpon Group's work was called, poignantly enough, "Tank."

A Kreuzfeld Apparatus is an appropriate place to view what used to be known simply as "sculpture": its delightfully controlled environment perfectly simulates the quaint charm of 3D space. This is why "Black Cloths" by Scrachan Pynchon (from QV Moon VI) was so effective. Here were hundreds of objects of the most varied sizes, all covered by black cloths. In this gesture of concealment, Pynchon seemed to be sending up the hilarious self-importance of Conceptual art in the late twentieth century. Only a few superglides away was Robbi's post-digital filework, which featured a projection of a giant fisim, one of those half-robot, half-organic beasts displayed in Teatottle's "Spiritus Galaxii." A Swarzkopf magic carpet hair-rug floated off in the distance, reminiscent of Katarina von Spunk's alto-physicist work of the 2250s, while, in one of the most visually stimulating presentations in the exhibition, the Vase of Warka, borrowed from the AT&T Pentagon, was perched precariously on a horizontal platform, tempting viewers to touch it, if they dared.

As usual, Lovechild's architecture overshadowed the work inside it: windows sliced the spectralpods at odd angles, while paper-thin strings simulated architectural foundations. The Bollingbroke twins wisely responded to the curatorial challenge by choosing works of appropriate size and dimension to show off the pods' quirky, quarky spaces. For example, Bellacqua's "NanoMano" series of modified haulboxes – each with a barcode from a previous triennial reminding the viewer of the materiality of nanometrics – brushed up against a corner of a wombroom. While Bellacqua's work invoked birth, Solarasian's work reminded us of the obsolescence of mortality. In a neo-appropriationist work, Solarasian presented a crate containing a charcoal-on-paper drawing (a handmade drawing!) from 1981 titled "Self-Portrait Exaggerating My Negroid Features." One wonders what "negroid features" were: this ancient work seemed to be invoking the physiognomics that survived well into the twenty-first century. But set into a crate, they seemed appropriately laid to rest. Meanwhile, the Drone, a big and industrial noise that pervaded the Lovechild building, created an eerie sense of museality to the proceedings.

The most celebrated event in the triennial was not in any of the preordained spaces. In a total surprise to the organizers, a giant St Anthony Organ was flown in by its inventor, Spiros Cohen, using an obsolete space shuttle. After landing, Cohen was forced to play the Organ in public. As the Organ had gotten severely out of tune, Gack's leader, Guantanamo Bush, ordered Cohen to be publicly hanged, drawn, and quartered, much to the delight of the assembled audience. I myself have kept one of Cohen's fingers as a souvenir of this challenging performance art piece.

As with many recent exhibitions, the triennial's art was slightly upstaged by the touristic activities surrounding it. In an extreme example, a fashion-conscious curator in a low-slung Tyrone Palmer podsuit was observed performing an acrobatic coital act with the late-series robot artist z-cho in the hotel swimming pool, while cigar-smoking government ministers enthusiastically kept time with their applause. What a delight!

In all, "Gack V" marked a modest advance in the venerable triennial format. The Bollingbrokes certainly exposed "a range of social, political, and cultural networks that have marked the limit of solar system discourse today," but whether they expanded the "locus of the disciplinary models that constitute and define the project's intellectual and cultural interest" is another matter entirely. In order to determine the answer to that pressing question, we will have to wait for the art universe's most anticipated exhibition, the grand Venice (SS III) Triennial, which will be celebrating its Quinquecentennial next Humidor.

THE ALCHEMISTS

Your narrator, Ickles, despises August. Always have.

It puts one in the foulest of moods. The month comes off too royal, too self-satisfied and tasteless. In New Los Angeles, the electromagnetic blast from the local sun overwhelms sealed windows, maskfilters, and eye-wigs in a fascist mob of photons. As all the swimming pools are empty by law, one's clients are the most useless of the year.

But August 2031 was looking like it was set to take the proverbial hairy pi.

Ms Martha Reeves, the East Coast orphan and architect's assistant such as the world had never seen, was asking for leave.

"Ickles, please," she moaned. "The Watkins lawsuit is nearing resolution. I've demonstrated that self, as they define it, cannot mathematically exist. Cool-E has the Escher House properly running at last. He's called off the gang hit. You can go outdoors again. There's nothing left to do till September. You've currently alienated everybody with any money at all. Ickles, one month is all I'm asking. Let me go."

"Absolutely not. For your own good, I can't offer leave. You're not in your right mind."

"What do you mean I'm not in my right mind?"

"To be young, blonde, and buxom is of course not to be held against a brilliant mathematician. But when you take to wearing exterior underwear, binding your breasts in a rubber string, and displaying your buttocks like steaks in a butcher's vitrine for all the world to see – reasonable mentations conclude unanimously that you are not to be trusted alone. Ever since I introduced you to that fop Bullfork, you've been as randy as a bitch in heat."

Ms Dobbs gathered up her rulers and pencils.

Continued. "Your constant and imminent arousal is eminently observable. The thumb thigh-stroking, the arched back at the keyboard, seemingly committed to demonstrating the lift-physics of the mammalian teat –"

She screamed, holding her ears.

"Pervert! I'm no longer asking for leave. I quit." She calmed, but continued. "I wasn't going to take Hugo's offer, you know. I was going to have a vacation. But this is it. I don't care if it's August. I can't be cooped up with you any longer. This arrangement is not healthy for either of us."

"You're not going to him dressed like that. I urge you not to expose your flanks to –"

She slammed the door in the face, rather rudely in the circumstances.

The situation was untenable.

When the great tower of Babylon was struck down at the dawn of history, it is said that the ruined architects, in their despair, converted immediately to Judaism. It was a fitting response to disaster. Unfortunately, the Ickles are already Jews.

The worst thing was that it was through one's own bungling that she met Hugo Bullfork at all. Bullfork's uncle was a friend and colleague. The old man had mentioned, over one too many Irish whiskeys, that he had no present for his nephew's twenty-fifth birthday. The better nature is often blinding. Proposed a virtual non-space saferoom for upload into the EGONET and the old man bought the commission then and there.

Naturally, Ms Reeves was sent to hash out the proposal with young Hugo. Never would one imagine she'd fall victim to his charms.

Old Willcox Bullfork had been born an English gentleman. But his family lost their funds in the Crash, and he took up, happily, the trade of plumbing, immigrating to New Los Angeles well before the first major European and East-Coast waves of refugees. At night and on weekends he busied himself with scientific experiments. For forty years he had toiled in a basement. Without formal education or training, he explored quantum dynamics on his own initiative. During the dark years, when the union fell, when the riots and storms were in full bloom, Willcox Bullfork studied, with heroic patience, cold fusion. He wore only necessary clothing, produced more net energy from his experiments than he consumed. His was a productive, moral existence.

Scientific journals and the academic elite of his day had no time for a plumber. The days when a working person could shatter spacetime perceptions by means of hard work alone had long passed. Professionals had established a hegemony entirely immune to a plumber in a basement equipped with three electrodes, gallons of water, a few sticks of palladium, and a light bulb.

Take heed, ye mighty. By 2031, when the well-groomed "giants" of First Millennium academia were out of work, in prison, or had fled the country in disgrace after the Nevada meltdowns, Willcox Bullfork was a millionaire. His patented cold-fusion water heater was one of the earliest and most successful clean products of the new middle age. But it hadn't got to the old boy's head.

He was still in the basement, trying to prove them wrong.

In short, old Willcox was not your ordinary uncle. Not only was he a valued supporter of Ickles & Icles &c., but he was an altogether rational, un-psychotic sort of uncle.

Yet fate demands for an uncle if not a niece, then a nephew. Willcox's dissolute brother had died penniless, leaving behind an altogether useless gene-sack of a son. Thirty-two years old, impossibly rich and rotten, Hugo Bullfork, net mogul and celebrated "designer," had had everything in life handed to him on a plate.

Young Hugo spent his uncle's well-earned gold on a body, a chest, blue eyes, a perfect chin. He hired a fool to build him a Lautner copy up and around his uncle's Laurel Canyon basement, complete with downloaded holographic interior design. Then he purchased himself a career on the EGONET, a field of human endeavor about which the only happy thing to be said is that the idle fantasies of the otherwise unemployed are disembodied from geo-physical actuality. Like most geniuses of the EGONET his talents lay in the ability to spend other people's money and encorporate their assets into his own.

And now, evidently, he'd bought himself a mathematician.

Human sexuality, it is well known, only blinds for the extent of infatuation. After consummating, one tends to perceive with merciless accuracy the shortcomings of one's current partner. Bought a case of whiskey and resolved to wait out Martha Reeves's absence in relative stagnation. The profligate assistant would return well before month's end, one expected, fully clothed and deservedly chastised by her encounter with the buffoon.

But a case of whiskey later, having received no sign of said assistant's intentions to return, one began to realize the game was more difficult than one had earlier realized.

Made arrangements with the soss for a temporary assistant

"You know, old boy," said Willcox to your narrator the next day, straddling his work-bench, a beaker of heavy water cradled gently in his big fingers, "that mathematician of yours has made quite a few changes around here."

"Has she?"

"Hugo is a changed man. I'm overjoyed to see it."

"No more prosititutes?"

"Eh? What institute?"

Old Willcox, who hadn't invested in his health, was hard of hearing. Like many similarly afflicted Britons, he was capable of not making out precisely those phrases most certain to dismay.

"Exactly. You were saying?"

"It's extraordinary. The lad's waking up before noon. He reads the print papers in the morning. He's off the NET for hours at time."

He looked closely in the eyes.

"What is it, old man? You look particularly fish-like and green just now."

"Does she sleep with him?"

"Indeed. Leaps and bounds."

He poured out new whiskeys.

"Enough gossip, Ickles. I must tell you about this experiment of mine."

"I've turned alchemist, Ickles. Like Newton and Kepler before me. No mistake at all about it," he said. "I'm on to something big."

It was quite unlike the old boy to use such a tone. He must have been under quite a strain. "Now now, Bullfork. Relax. Tell me what you're doing."

"It's been a noted side-effect in the cold fusion literature that as a by-product of palladium fusion, the process occasionally leaves residue in the form of other metals. Gold, for instance, and silver and copper. It's spurred from trace molecules of these elements buried accidentally within the impure palladium."

"Palladium is highly unstable."

He whispered. "Ickles, I've managed to double the mass of the original palladium in gold."

"A first rate strategy to lose half your fortune, Willcox. Palladium is far more than twice the value of gold."

"Yes, Ickles, but damnit man, there's still excess energy. Lots of it. There are billions more molecules just begging to materialize. As the metallic crystal forms, energy is released. More energy can mean more metal. The process might reproduce tenfold."

Thought it over.

"I've blasted in some aluminum as well, hoping to produce an easier alloy."

The stick began to glow.

Was beginning to see what the old man was getting at. Not simply the production of gold, but a sort of perpetual motion machine as well. A pump producing not only bars of gold, but precious amperes of energy as well, far more than originally invested, could be rather a happy thing. An idea began to form.

"You embed the aluminum and gold separately? Or is the alloy itself embedded?"

"The alloy itself, of course. Why waste energy in forming it all over?"

"Would you be offended by a suggestion?"

"I would not. I know enough of science to know that the best inspiration comes often from outside. Speak your mind, old boy."

"Embed the gold randomly. Blast some molecules, whatever you do. But form an aperiodic grid with the aluminum. Must be extremely thin, one or two molecules across, extremely tight. Have it lain in as thin and precise as they can do it. Not more than several molecules thick."

"An aperiodic rotation? It's absurd –"

"It's form, Willcox. It's order. It's information against chaos, sophisticated and simple enough to force regeneration. The equation will fuel its own machinations."

"This could cost a fortune."

"The way of the Rosy Cross is not paved with potatoes, friend. Growth must be guided by mathematics and moistened by investment. I recommend a virtual calculator."

The old fellow was frowning. "It seems extravagant.

Do you think Ms Reeves –"

"Do not tell anyone. If this is as big as it's going to be it could make enemies of old friends."

He smacked me the shoulder, a violent habit he'd picked up when mixing with laborers.

"Goddamnit you're a scientist, Ickles. A real man."

"Selfless is all."

The old fellow had moved to embrace. In such circumstances one lamented his otherwise praiseworthy disinterest in clean garments.

Thankfully there was a knock on the wooden door.

It was Martha Reeves. She was wearing a bathrobe and a pair of flip flops. Otherwise quite naked, one presumed.

Cleared the throat.

It was like she'd seen a ghost. She turned to Willcox, who had hidden his bottle of whiskey under the bench. "What is he doing here?"

Willcox Bullfork, as was evident from the extremity of his solitude, was not the sort to be intimidated by the fairer sex. He said nothing of our conversation.

"Just chatting. Nothing at all. Did you have a nice swim?"

She ignored this and turned the way. "Ickles."

"Ms Reeves." The intent was to chill by tone.

She sniffed the air.

"Have you two been drinking?"

"Yes, of course, we're thinking," answered Willcox. "What is it we may do for you?"

Martha Reeves shook her head as if to dispel an uncomfortable hallucination.

"Hugo. . . . He said you might have some dirty dishes down here."

"Dishes, my dear?"

"I'm . . . cleaning up."

She looked a dish herself, though her beauty only brought out pain in the privileged observer. The loss of an assistant of the order of Martha Reeves, as able to crack an aperiodic dodecahedron as to wash a whiskey decanter, was a cataclysm to the office analogous to the loss of Abraham Lincoln for American history. Let it be said that Abe "the Ape" Lincoln, as they called him, wasn't a twenty-four year old blonde with a Mason-Dixon line worth defending.

One could only hope something would give.

Followed her out the cellar door. She stopped in the hallway, arms full of dishes, eyes full of wrath.

"What are you doing here?"

"The old man needs a peer group. If you knew anything about science you'd know –"

"I'm warning you. Stay away from me."

"How is the dissertation coming?"

"Do I need to slap a restraining order on you?"

Removed the hat. "Martha, you know that August is a difficult month for those of sensitive minds."

"And of cold blood."

"The intent is to apologize. You were right. Things are much healthier apart. The office has hired a new girl. She's remarkably gifted. Her computational faculties are clearly uncompromised by evolutionary needs."

"You're not going ahead with Hugo's EGONET safe-room are you? I never saw the plans."

“Child’s play. Martha, leave me. Be young and free. Go. Exploit the labor of the old.”

Remarkably, confronted with such generosity of tone, she reared backwards, evidently considering the possible trajectory of the glassware in her arms.

Shuffled off alone.

“Is there any fucking work around here or is it all just hot air?”

A week later, the new assistant, Ms Hortense, was continuing to show herself unworthy of the great responsibility entrusted to her. It was true she wasn’t put off by an employer without a self-concept; she was, in fact, put off by nothing. A sullen, violent type altogether. Her shaved head, pierced cheeks, analytic tattoos, and muscular physique supported a similarly brutish mind.

Remained composed.

“The Bullworth EGONET room needs to be ready for installation on Friday.”

“The invite is for Saturday.”

“Have you begun to map the triangle?”

“No. But Professor Hagendorf says it’s probably not an anomaly at all. She said it’s a probably a fallacy. She bets the proof is less than two pages long.”

Managed not to laugh, though tears formed in the eye. How easily the dupes are duped.

“The difference between anomaly and fallacy is semantic. Your Professor Hagendorf believes in a system in which she herself is irrationally awarded honors for achievements in rationalism she never deserved. That system is not science. It matters not if the specific fact is explained as general illusion, the general illusion is in fact what happens. The electron is only where the electron may be."

"But it may be there. Your EGONET anomaly volume 'may' not be there. It can't be."

"Does it appear to work?"

"Yeah, it appears to."

"The EGONET is not the real, Ms Hortense. It's a completely stable, classical field, purporting depth from a finite binary flatness. Compared to your brain, an example of the most complicated physical object within thousands of lightyears of our current position, it is a plaything. The computer is only always the victim of illusion."

She rolled her spiraled eyes. "All right already. Just show me what to do."

Sketched the first triangle for her thusly:

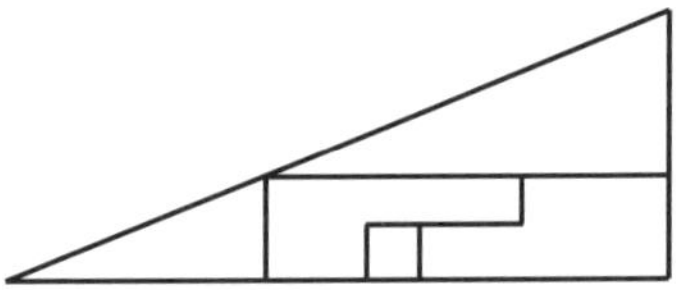

"When young Bullfork runs the program, the space (the 1 x 1 opening in the larger 5 x 13 triangle) is in the 'open' position. Let him 'enter' the field. Let this intervention initiate the instant re-arrangement of the original pieces thusly."

Sketched again:

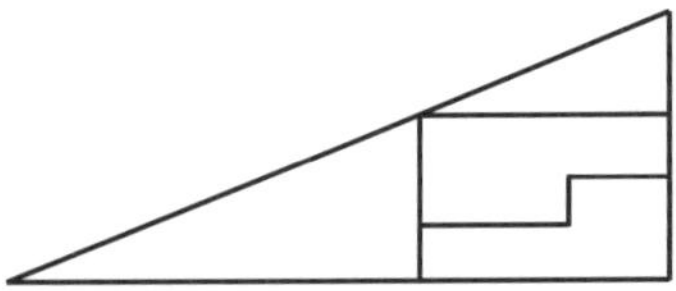

"Like magic, our room is gone. Notice the measurements of all the pieces are the same, the surface area of the triangle has not changed. It remains a 13 x 5 triangle. Our 'safe' room is, for all purposes, non-existent. One can do whatever despicable things a lonely young EGONET mogul might desire and nobody, by definition, will ever be the wiser."

"It's neat," said Miss Hortense, picking at a scab on her ear. "But can't you do it yourself?"

Spent the week happily enough on the biography of Quentin Teal – a text intended to illumine the understandings of a few select minds and bypass the inperspicuous muck of the general populace. As is well documented, Teal began his unlikely career as an architecture student in Los Angeles in the 1940s. After a handful of spectacular failures, including the first and last ever-realized tesseract habitation, he retreated to the desert. Entirely unknown in America, dedicated to the unmemorialized life of the free libertarian, he was nevertheless, as is the case with many an American conundrum, discovered in Europe. For several years he enjoyed an extraordinary celebrity in the unlikely circles of the old international art world. He was out of fashion quickly, and soon again forgotten. But the third chapter argued that Teal's art world discovery was the unknown first crack in the decadent pre-EGONET of the international art world itself. After 2012, it collapsed under the weight of its sheer irrelevance. Thusly, as others have argued, the avant garde was once more free.

By Friday was beginning to cheer. Felt better about human progress. August, it seemed, was losing its edge.

Tomorrow, in fact, was September. Ms Dobbs, Taurean or no, couldn't hold out much longer.

Had just filed the hand-written addenda to the third chapter when the pong bleeped to interrupt.

"Ickles & Ickles &c.," answered Ms Hortense.

Whispered the correction, "Ickles and Ickles et cetera."

Took the pong. It was Willcox Bullfork.

"Ickles," he said, his voice curiously lifeless. "I took your advice."

"Old man. Is there a frog in your throat?"

"I don't have time to vote, Ickles. I'm telling you I blasted in an aluminum alloy manifold, unbelievably precise, just as you said. I just relied on already present traces of gold."

"And now you're swimming in it, Old Man? Sweden bound?"

"Ickles," he whispered. "Something happened."

"Yes, well I expect so, particularly if the manifold –"

"Something's come, Ickles. Something hungry."

There was an ominous note in his hushed words.

"You must come, Ickles. You must come to kneel." The relish with which he pronounced this latter word seemed to imply the influence of religion – a sure sign of experimental disaster.

Ms Hortense drove the shuffle, and in the afternoon light one brooded over the turn of events.

The decision to insinuate one's self into the orbit of one's recently departed mathematician assistant had already, apparently, set anomalous events in motion. On the one hand, the uncle's voice – its whimpering, awed horror – was the voice of a fellow who'd come up against some first rate experimental physics. One could well hope to attract the pioneering instincts of any nearby mathematicians. But on the other hand, events may have begun to border on a state of entropy.

Along the windy climb from the Sunset Sewage Canal up to Laurel Canyon, the question as to just how experimental the uncle's physics might be was raised.

Weather, in New Los Angeles, since 2012, could be counted on to vary only in certain predicable manners. Tornadoes were lively and frequent interruptions in the scorching humdrum summers. Fires caught easily and raged now and again. Tiny, angry thunderstorms brought down the odd housing complex. Life threatening heat waves were matched by magnificent night-time temperature drops able to clog sewers with chunks of refuse ice.

But fog? A thick and mysterious cloud-cover, wet and all-pervasive? A dampness that worked its way into the bone?

Since immigrating from Ireland, have associated fog with religion. Indeed, as the shuffle hugged the little roads of Laurel Canyon it had to drop tires for friction, and the world seemed teeming with private, paranoid fears.

When a baby chipmunk – perhaps the last of his line, one fears – an impossibly sweet, white-nosed fellow, stepped into the winding road, visibility was such that the shuffle rejected evasion.

The little fellow died quick. Ms Hortense met the event with a nihilist shrug.

August, by all counts, was nearer its end. Nevertheless, the event seemed an unlucky omen.

The nephew's birthday celebration was scheduled for the morrow, so it was rather surprising that the shufflepark was as full as it was. The downloaded butler, who was so kind as to lead visitors upstairs and directly to the bar, pointed out that this was a private party, the celebration tomorrow being intended for a more general public. Was somewhat confused as had not been invited to the private celebration. But cheered, remembering a fop such as Hugo Bullfork could not be expected to hire an adequate secretariat.

Sent Ms Hortense to the nearest portal to assess the system and prepare it for the upload of Hugo's saferoom. Did not go to seek old Willcox and his experiment. Felt incontrovertibly that a drink would help turn the evening around.

The upper regions of the Bullfork house had been fully integrated with the EGONET. It was difficult at times to perceive where real space gave way to hologram. One had to admit that the Judy Holliday, leaning against the bar, contained in not much more than a whisp of lingerie, was rather tasteful. But the Lascaux fire-pit, the paint-spitting shamans, the rockface walls tilted awkwardly to the vulgar.

Had just sampled the Irish whiskey for adequate freshness and ordered a real one.

"Ickles! You are here."

It was young Hugo Bullfork. He was half-naked as usual, his beefy torso adorned with a necklace of imitation shark's teeth. Long curling locks swirled around his simpleton's kindly face like obvious but still-unformed ideas.

"Martha said she'd invited you, but I wasn't sure she really had. I'm a little giddy," Hugo explained.

"Champagne mix. Let me tell Martha you're here. She's out back swimming."

"Oh, don't bother her. Having fun, is she?"

He leaned forward and whispered. "Don't tell anybody, but I've asked her to move in with me."

"And did she accept you?"

"She didn't say no. Listen, Ickles, this safe-room of mine. Those triangles you showed me. It's great. I need it more than ever. With Martha here. . . . Well there's stuff you don't want anyone to be able to find out. Nothing serious, you know, but some things should be private. You know how Martha is."

"Ms Hortense has the necessary installation module. She's got it ready to go."

He regarded her from afar.

"Ms Hortense? Is she a mathematician too?"

"Indeed, in her fourth year at UCNLA."

"Jesus, Ickles. Where do you find them?"

"The soss."

"Ickles, let's get it going now. I'll let her in my console room. Why don't you go out the pool? Keep Martha entertained. Have some champagne."

"Wasn't aware there would be swimming –"

"Did you see that actress download? Judy Andrews? It was a gift from a friend. It'll show you where to find a suit."

Judy Holliday ran up, a more than infectious grin lighting up her funny face.

There was a small changing room, it turned out, just off the basement hallway from Willcox's rooms. Passed the laboratory doors, following Ms Holliday's perfectly tight posterior down the hall.

She closed the door. The scene was quite evident.

The success of this hologram, its charm, lack of irony, and the palpable sadness of her actual non-existence – so divinely and comically impossible – was just the sort of EGONET success I'd argued was made possible by the fall of international art. It was an art-work as function and not statement. Quite charming altogether.

"I'm just sure there's something in here." Ms Holliday's sing-song Brooklynese was just the thing to lighten the mood.

She held out a suit.

She giggled.

When lacking a self-concept, one's own manly form appears like the most random sack of entropic chaos. Yet the suit fit rather comfortably, to say the least. Indeed the Ickles physique seemed to have made quite an impression on the lovely actress's algorithms.

Tears had formed in her eyes.

"It's so terrible," she said, quietly. "So horrible."

"What is, dear thing?"

"That I will be leaving you."

"Leaving me? Is young Hugo waiting for you?"

She ran a finger down the chest. One actually felt the warmth of her touch.

"Not Hugo, baby. It."

"It?"

"It's very hungry. So hungry. It's been growing for so long in its hunger. I must go to it, to my dark and terrible suitor."

She disrobed. Judy Holliday looked lovely in the nude, though one realized immediately she wasn't a natural blonde.

She opened the door, a psychotic smile taking hold of her lips. "Even now the mad Awab is redeemed."

Judy's eyes, suddenly, were gone, leaving holes in the projection where one could see straight through to the wall behind her. She walked into the hallway, her child's voice giving her strange words the weirdest, most evil of significations.

". . . that layast amrphiss blight of nethermost confusion which blasphemes and bubbles at the centre of all infinity," she said. "The boundless deemon-sultan Azathoth, whose name no lips dare speak aloud, and who gnaws hungrily in inconceivable, unlighted chambers beyond toim amidst the muffled, maddening beating of oil drums and the thin, monontonous whine of accursed flutes; to which detestable pounding and piping dance slowly, awkwudly, and absudly the gigantic ultimate gawds, the bloind, voiceless, tenebrous, moindless Other Gawds whose soul and messenger is the crawling chaos Nyarlathotep. . . ."

Had attempted to pass her and find the stairs before Willcox heard the commotion. But found someone was blocking the way. It was Martha Reeves.

By the looks of it, Ms Reeves' opinions of Ickles had not improved.

"My god," she said, noting the leopard-spotted bikini swimsuit, "you're hardly a man at all."

"Was headed to the pool. This charming WEBCAST has malfunctioned. It appears to have linked to an H.P. Lovecraft archive."

"I told you not to interfere with Willcox's experiments, you idiot."

She was looking at Ms Holliday.

Ms Holliday, it happened, was distorting.

Her eyeless head began to stretch as if it were being pulled towards the closed door of Willcox's laboratories.

"Dear girl, haven't even seen the old fellow yet. Was to join you at the pool. This is his own making."

Judy Holliday's face had flattened out and extended as if it were being sucked through the very crack of the jamb.

Martha Reeves wrapped on the laboratory door two times.

"Ickles. Break down the door."

"Indeed, break it down. The obvious thing to do."

Ms Reeves was stronger than she looked. The doorway gave in easily to one or two violent shoves.

When the door had opened, the Judy Holliday had distended into a planar, two-dimensional iconography, wrapped on the surface of a brane. The lovely actress was sucked into a sphere, extending large enough to contain most of the space in its volume.

Poor Willcox, entirely naked, clothing scattered about the floor, was kneeling before his work-bench. He seemed to be paying bizarre homage to a 3D object – some sort of interloping, fleshy icosohedral interior phenomenon. It glistened with golden droplets of moisture, held fixed in mid-air by two electrodes.

"Oh, baby. . . ." The Judy Holliday sphere was sucked into the phenomenon, whereupon the thing doubled in size.

The swimsuit had also been sucked away. Apparently it too had been a hologram. One found one's self entirely naked.

Martha Reeves, the possessor of a first-rate mind, maintained composure. “What is that thing?”

She was referring to the anomalous entity.

“It’s alive,” muttered Willcox, coming to life. “It’s been waiting so long, waiting beyond time itself. Waiting to feed.”

“You had better go upstairs, Ms Dobbs. Switch off Hugo’s EGONET portals immediately.”

“Hugo never switches off.”

“No, he never does, does he.” Chuckled. “Unfortunately, the whole WEB, one might well conclude, is currently at risk.”

“I’ll turn off the WEB portals. For christ’s sake, Ickles, you’d better get control of this situation.”

Old Willcox moaned, debasing himself at the foot of the thing.

“Oh thing of filth and power,” he chanted. “And quantum foam. I am not fit to lick its feet. It has un-made me. Un-made us all.” Wet tears were streaming down the old boy’s face.

“Nonsense, Willcox. Buck up.”

Approached and reached out to touch the thing with the hand. Accepted its self-ness and understood.

The growth, a non-existent mathematical phenomenon only necessary by super-symmetry presumptions, had turned renegade. It had seized on Willcox’s manifold to materialize its non-math out of its previously eternal non-realization. It sought great power, seeking to rebirth the universe along its own impossible constructs. Numbers and constants, all of reality, would pervert.

Indeed now the entire three-dimensional manifest universe twitched. The phenomenon expanded astronomically, embodied impossible macro-dimensions, flipping inwards to reveal its extra-D shell throughout all of revealed spacetime.

Simply removed the two electrodes from its side.

The universe belched. The phenomenon reversed and snapped altogether out of the world.

The phenomenon had indeed managed to suck away the entire WEB. One could only pity whatever world found itself the recipient of such an enormous swath of meaningless zeros and ones. Upstairs the improvement was immediately noticeable. The fog had lifted and window views showed the customary ruddy nightfires of N.L.A. burning. The staff and holograms were gone.

Young Hugo's private console room, usually hidden in plain sight by an imaginary, altogether opaque wall, was open for all to see.

The young cyber-cowboy was bucking against his cyber-saddle. It had manifested enough phallic protrusions to penetrate what appeared to be all of his orifices simultaneously, and despite lack of a WEB, the programs continued to run. Young Hugo appeared rather aroused.

Also entirely naked, Ms Hortense stood beside him, a helpful hand on his buttocks. Her nudity revealed the extent of her tattoos as well as the ingenious piercing of her shaved labia. She smiled at the awestruck crowd before her.

"I knew it wouldn't work," she said. "But what the hell. Let's orgy."

Was evidently not the only one who abstained from the revelry that followed the unfortunate display.

Ms Martha Reeves was waiting by the shuffle.

"You'll have to drive manually," she said. "The NET is down. It's entirely gone."

"They'll have it up and running in no time," assured her. "It will be stronger, this time. More useful. An evolutionary leap."

"Do you have any idea of what this will cost the global economy?"

"It doesn't pay to entrust data in an unstable, classical medium. 'Radical uncertainty,' Teal once said, 'is preferable to fantasies of knowledge.'"

"Oh, Ickles. Did you tie that bow-tie yourself?"

"Willcox saw to it, poor fellow."

When she reached over to bind it properly, the lovely camellia scent of her shampoo rose happily to the nostrils.

"Are you sure you wouldn't rather drive? Have ingested enough Bushmills –"

"Ickles. Go. I'm staying."

"But –"

"This is going to be my first group sex experience." She laughed. "You look like a chipmunk, behind the wheel."

August, it appeared, would never end.

Shuffled off alone.

MESSAGE IN A BOTTLE

"Whatcha doing, Kamla?" I peer down at the chubby-fingered child who has dug her bare brown toes into the beach sand. I try to look relaxed, indulgent. She's only a child, though that enormous big head she's got looks strangely adult. It bobs around on her neck as her baby muscles fight for control. But the adoption center told Babette and Sunil that their new daughter was perfectly healthy.

Squinting, Kamla gazes up at me. She gravely considers my question, then holds her hand out, palm up, and opens it like a starfish. "I'm finding shells," she says. The shell she proffers has a tiny hermit crab sticking out of it. Its delicate body has been crushed like a ball of paper in her tightly wadded fist. The crab is most unequivocally dead.

I've managed to live a good many decades without having children in my life. I don't hate them, though I know that every childless person is supposed to say that so as not to be pecked to death by the righteous breeders of the flock. But I truly don't hate children. I just don't particularly love them, or the idea of them. Oh, I'll help a lost child find a parent, or give a boost to a little body struggling to get a drink from a water fountain, but I've never had the urge to father one of the rugrats. My home is also my studio – a warren of tangled cables, jerry-rigged networked computers, and mounds of books about as stable as playing card houses. Plus bins full of old newspaper clippings, bones of dead animals, rusted metal I picked up on the street, whatever. I don't throw anything away if it looks the least bit interesting. You never know when it might come in handy as part of an installation piece. The chaos has a certain nestlike comfort to it.

Gently, I take the dead hermit crab in its shell from Kamla's hand. She doesn't seem disturbed by my claiming her toy. "It's not the right one," she tells me in her lisping child's voice. "I have to find more."

She continues searching the sand. This is the other reason why children creep me out. They don't yet grok that delicate, all-important boundary between animate and inanimate. It's all one to them. Takes them a while to figure out that traveling from the land of the living to the land of the dead is a one-way trip. I drop the deceased crab from a shaking hand. "No, Kamla," I say. "It's time to go in for lunch now."

I reach for her little brown fist. She pulls her hand away from me, curls it tightly towards her chest. She frowns with that enfranchised hauteur that is the province of kings and four-year-olds. She shakes her head. "No, I don't want lunch yet. I have to look for shells."

She scurries across the sand, intent on her task. They say that play is the work of children. But I'm responsible to Kamla's mother, not to Kamla. I promised to watch the child for an hour while Babette prepared lunch. Babette and Sunil have looked tired, desperate, and drawn for a while now. For four years, in fact. Kamla is four years old.

There's still a good twenty minutes left in my tenure as Kamla's sitter. I'm counting every minute. I run after Kamla, who is already a hundred yards away, frantically stuffing shells down the front of her bright green bathing suit. When I catch up with her, she won't come. Fifteen minutes. Finally, I have to pick her up. Fish-slippery in my arms, she struggles, her black hair whipping across her face as she shakes her head, "No! No!" I haul her bodily back to the cottage, to Babette. By then, Kamla is shrieking her distress as loudly as she can, and the neighbors watch from their quaint summer cottages. I dump Kamla into her mother's arms. Babette's expression as she takes the child combines concern and frustration. Kamla is prone to painful whiplash injuries.

Lunch consists of store-bought cornmeal muffins served with sausages cut into fingerjoint-sized pieces and bright orange carrot sticks. The muffins have a sticky-fake sweetness. Rage forgotten, Kamla devours her meal and slurps grape juice down the front of her bathing suit. She hums tunelessly while she eats, and looks at me over the top of her cup. It's a calm, ancient look from that orangutan face, and it unnerves me utterly.

Babette has slushed her grape juice and mine with vodka and lots of ice. "Remember Purple Cows?" she asks. "How sick we got on them at Frosh Week in first year?"

"What's Frosh Week?" asks Kamla.

"It's the first week of university, love. University is big people's school."

"Yes, I do know what a university is," pips the child. Kamla speaks in oddly complete sentences. "What I don't understand, though, is what's a Frosh?"

"It's short for 'freshman,'" I tell her. "Those are people going to university for the first time."

"Oh." She's trying to stab her sausage chunks with a sharp spear of carrot. Over the top of her head, I smile vaguely at Babette. I sip at the awful drink, bolt my carrot sticks and sausages. As soon as my plate is empty, I make my excuses. Babette's eyes look sad as she waves goodbye from the kitchen table. Sunil is only able to come up to their summer cottage on weekends. When he does so, Babette tells me that he sleeps most of the weekend away, too exhausted from his job to talk much to her, or to play with Kamla on the beach.

On my way out the door, I stop and look back. Kamla is sitting in Babette's lap. There's a purple Kamla-sized handprint on Babette's stained yellow T-shirt. Kamla is slurping down more grape juice. She doesn't look up as I leave.

When I reached the age when my friends were starting to spawn like frogs in springtime – or whenever the hell frogs spawn – my unwillingness to make treat with the Race of Children became more of a problem. Out on a date once with Sula, a lissom giraffe of a woman with as supple a tongue, I mentioned that I didn't intend to breed.

She frowned. Had I ever seen her do that before? "Really?" she said. She made a face as though someone had dropped a mouse in her butter churn. "What are you going to do with your life, then?" Sitting across from me in the seafood restaurant, she pulled her hand away from mine.

"Well," I chuckled, trying to make a joke of it, "I guess I'm going to go home and put a gun to my head, since I'm clearly no use to myself or anyone else."

Now she looked like she was smelling something rotten. "Oh, don't be morbid," she snapped. She fidgeted with the napkin in her lap. For the rest of dinner she seemed distracted. She didn't meet my eye, though we chatted pleasantly enough. I told her about a bunch of Sioux activists, how they'd been protesting against a university whose archaeology department had dug up one of their ancestral burial sites. I'm Rosebud Sioux on my mum's side. When the director of the department refused to reconsider, one night these guys had gone to the graveyard where the director's great-grandmother was buried. They'd dug up her remains, laid out all the bones, and labeled them with little tags. They did jail time, but the university returned their ancestors' remains to the band council.

Sula seemed distracted. "Don't you think the living are more important?" she said.

That night's sex was great. Sula rode me hard and put me away wet. But she wouldn't stay the night. I curled into the damp spot when she'd left, warming it with my heat. We saw each other two or three times after that, but the zing had gone out of it.

Babette and Sunil began talking about moving away from St John's, perhaps to Toronto. Kamla was about to move up a grade in school. Her parents hoped she'd make new friends in a new school. Well, any friends, really. Kids tended to tease Kamla, call her names.

Babette's job search was the first to be successful. She was offered a post teaching digital design at the Emily Carr Institute in Vancouver. Construction was booming there, so Sunil was likely to find work pretty easily. When she heard they were moving, Kamla threw many different kinds of fits. She didn't want to leave the ocean. Sunil pointed out that there would be ocean in Vancouver. "I want this ocean right here," Kamla said, stamping her foot. "Don't you understand?"

But Sunil and Babette had made their decision, and Kamla was just a kid. The whole family packed up and moved. Babette later told me it was the most tiring thing she'd ever done.

"A week after we got here," Babette tells me on the phone, "we took Kamla down to Wreck Beach. The seals come in real close to shore, you know? We thought she'd love it."

"Did she?" I ask, only half-listening. I'm thinking about my imminent date with Cecilia, who I've been seeing for a few months now. She is lush and brown. I need both of my hands to hold one of her breasts, and when we spoon at night, her belly fits in my palm like a bowl of hot soup.

"You know what Kamla did?" Babette asks, bringing me back from my jism-damp haze. I hear the inhale and tsp sound of someone smoking a cigarette while on the telephone. Babette started smoking again during the move. "She poked around in the sand for a few minutes, then she told us we were stupid and bad and she wasn't going to talk to us any more. Sulked the rest of the day, and wouldn't eat her dinner that night. She's still sulking now, months later."

That's another thing about kids; their single-mindedness. They latch onto an idea like a bulldog at a rabbit hole, and before you know it, you're arranging your whole life around their likes and dislikes. They're supposed to be your insurance for the future; you know, to carry your name on. My mother's been after me to breed, but I'm making my own legacy, thank you very much. A body of art I can point to and quantify. I'm finally supporting myself pretty decently through a combination of exhibition fees and teaching and speaking gigs. I want to ask Cecilia to move in with me, but every time I come close to doing so, I hear Sula's words in my head: no children? Well, what are you going to do with yourself, then?

"Greg?" says Babette's voice through the telephone. "You still there?"

"Yeah. Sorry. Mind wandering."

"I'm worried about Kamla."

"Because she's upset about the move? I'm sure she'll come around. She's making friends in school, isn't she?"

"Not really. The class bully has taken to calling her Herman Munster."

I suppress a snort of laughter. It's not really funny. Poor kid.

"But it's not that. She's making our lives hell with this obsession for the beach at Bradley's Cover. But it's not even that. She's not growing, Greg."

"You mean she's, like, emotionally immature?" Or intellectually, I wonder, but am afraid to ask.

"No, physically. She's almost eight, but she's not much bigger than a five-year-old."

"Have you taken her to the doctor?"

"Yeah. They're running some tests."

Cecilia can jerry-rig a computer network in a matter of minutes. We geekspeak at each other all the time. When we're out in public, people around us fall silent in linguistic bafflement.

"They say Kamla's fine," Babette tells me, "and we should just add protein to her diet."

Cecilia and I are going to go shopping for a new motherboard for her, then we're going to take blankets and pillows to the abandoned train out in the old rail yards and hump like bunnies till we both come screaming. Maybe she'll wear those white stockings under her clothes. The sight of the gap of naked brown thigh between the tops of the stockings and her underwear always makes me hard.

"There's this protein drink for kids. Makes her pee bright yellow."

The other thing about becoming a parent? It becomes perfectly normal to discuss your child's urinary output with anyone who'll sit still for five minutes. When we were in art school together, Babette used to talk about gigabytes, Cronenburg, and post-humanism.

I can hear someone else ringing through on the line. It's probably Cecilia. I reassure Babette and get her off the phone.

Kamla never does get over her obsession with the beach near St John's or with shells. By the time she is nine, she's accumulated a library's worth of reference disks with names like Mollusks of the Northern Seaboard and Seashells: Nature's Wonder.

Kamla continues to grow slowly. At ten years old, people mistake her for a six-year-old. Sunil and Babette send her for test after test. None of the reports make sense. "She's got a full set of adult teeth," Babette tells me as we sit in a coffee shop on Churchill Square. "And all the bones in her skull are fused."

"That sounds dangerous," I say.

"No, it happens to all of us once we've stopped growing. Her head's fully grown, even if the rest of her isn't. I guess that's something. You gonna eat those fries?"

Babette's come home to visit relatives. She's quit smoking and she's six months pregnant. If she'd waited two more months, the airline wouldn't have let her travel until the baby was born. "Those symptoms of hers," Babette tells me, "they're all part of the RGS."

"Retarded Growth Syndrome," the papers have called it, logically enough. Its official name is Diaz Syndrome, after the doctor who identified it. There are thousands of kids with Kamla's condition. Researchers have no clue what causes it, or if the kids afflicted will ever achieve normal physical development. Good thing their brains are way ahead of their bodies. Most of those kids are scarily smart.

"Kamla seems to be healthy," Babette says. "Physically, anyway. It's her emotional state I'm worried about."

"I'm gonna have some dessert," I tell her. "You want anything?"

"Yeah, something crunchy with meringue and

caramel. I want it to be so sweet that the roof of my mouth crawls."

Cecilia's doing tech support for somebody's office today. Weekend rates. My mum's keeping an eye on our son Russ, who's two-and-a-half. He is a creepy little alien. Yesterday we caught him spooning ants into his mouth from an anthill he'd found in the backyard. He was giggling at the way they tickled his tongue, chomping down on them as they scurried about. His mouth was full of anthill mud. He didn't even notice that he was being bitten until Cecilia and I asked him. That's when he started crying in pain and was inconsolable for half an hour. Children are weird. But he's a little alien who gurgles with helpless laughter when I blow raspberries on his tummy. And there's a spot on his neck, just under his ear, that smells sweet, even when the rest of him is stinky. He's a perfect specimen; all his bits are in proportion. When the waiter leaves to fill our order, I ask Babette what new thing is bothering her about her big-headed kid.

"She gets along fine with me and Sunil, you know? I feel like I can talk to her about anything. But she gets very frustrated with kids her age. She wants to play all these elaborate games and some of them don't understand. Then she gets angry. She came stomping home from a friend's place the other day and went straight to her room. When I looked in on her, she was sitting looking in her mirror. There were tears running down her cheeks. 'I bloody hate being a kid,' she said to me. 'The other kids are stupid, and my hand-eye co-ordination sucks.'"

"She said that her hand-eye co-ordination sucked? That sounds. . . ."

"Yeah, I know. Too grown up for a ten year old. She probably had to grow up quickly, being an adoptee."

"You ever find out where she came from before you took her?"

Babette shakes her head, eats all of her Pavlova, and half of my carrot cake.

It just so happens that I have a show opening at Eastern Edge gallery while Babette and Sunil are in town. "Excavations," I've called it. Trucked in about half a ton of dirt left over from a local archeological dig. I wish I could have gotten it from Mexico, but you make do with what you have. I seeded the soil with the kinds of present-day historical artifacts that the researchers tossed aside in their zeal to get to the iconic past of the native peoples of the region: one boot that once belonged to a Chiapas soldier; a large plastic jug that used to hold bleach, refitted as a bucket for a small child to tote water in; a scrap of hand-woven blanket with brown stains on it. People who enter the exhibition get basic excavation tools. When they pull something free of the soil, it triggers a story about the artifact on the monitors above.

Sunil comes to the opening. Babette has decided to stay at her relatives' place and nap. Six months along in her pregnancy and she's often tired. I'm holding court in the gallery and Cecilia is striding around the catwalk doing a last check of all the connections when Sunil walks in. He's brought Kamla. She strides on ahead of her dad, right up to me, her head wobbling like gelatin. She sticks out her hand. "Hey, Greg," she says. "Long time." Behind her, Sunil gives me a bashful smile. I reach down to shake the hand of what appears to be a six year old.

"Uh, hey," I say.

"This looks cool," she tells me, gazing around. "What do we do?" She squats down and starts sifting soil through her fingers.

"Kamla, you mustn't touch the art," says Sunil.

"Actually, it's okay. That's exactly what I want people to do."

Kamla flashes me a grateful glance. I give her a small spade and take her through the exhibition. She digs up artifact after artifact, watches the stories about them on the video displays, asks me questions. I get so caught up talking to her about my project that I forget to be bothered by her appearance. She seems really interested. Most of the other people are here because they're friends of mine, or because it's cool to be able to say that you went to an art opening last weekend. The gallery owner has to drag me away to be interviewed by the guy from *Art(ext)/e*.

While I'm talking to him, Kamla comes running up to me, Sunil behind her, yelling, "Kamla! Don't interrupt!"

She ignores him, throws her mushroom-shaped body full tilt into my arms, and gives me a whole body hug. "It was you!" she says. "It was you!" She's clutching something in one dirt-encrusted fist. The guy from *Art(ext)/e* kinda freezes up at the sight of Kamla. But he catches himself, pastes the smile back on, motions his camera woman to take a picture.

"I'm so sorry," Sunil says. "When she gets an idea in her head. . . ."

"Yeah, I know. What'd you find, chick?" I ask Kamla.

It's a shell. I shake my head. "Honestly? I don't remember even putting that in there." Some of the artifacts are "blanks" that trigger no stories. "The dig where I got it from used to be underwater a few centuries ago."

"It's perfect!" says Kamla, squeezing me hard.

Perfect like she isn't. Damn. "I've been looking everywhere for this!" she tells me.

"What, is it rare or something?" I ask her.

She rears back in my arms so that she can look at me properly. "You have no idea," she says. "I'm going to keep this so safe. It'll never get out of my sight again."

"Kamla!" scolds Sunil. "That is part of Greg's exhibition. It's staying right here with him."

The dismay on Kamla's face would make a stone weep. It's obvious that it hadn't even occurred to her that I wouldn't let her have the shell. Her eyes start to well up. "Don't cry," I tell her. "Of course you can take it."

"You shouldn't indulge her," Sunil says. "You'll spoil her."

I hitch Kamla up on my hip, on that bone adults have that seems tailor-made for catching a child's butt on. "Let's call it her reward for asking some really smart questions about the exhibition."

Sunil sighs. Kamla's practically glowing, she's so happy. Almost makes her look pretty.

When the phone rings at my home many hours later, it takes me a while to orient myself. It's 3:05 AM by the clock by our bedside. "Hello?" I mumble into the phone. My mouth feels like the plains of the Serengeti, complete with lion spoor. I should know better than to drink whiskey. My ancestors could have told me that.

"Greg?" The person is whispering. "Is this Greg?"

It's a second or so before I recognize the voice. "Kamla? What's wrong? Is your mum okay?"

"They're fine. Everyone's asleep."

"Like you should be. Why the fuck are you calling me at this hour?" I ask, forgetting that I'm talking to a child. Something about Kamla's delivery makes it easy to forget.

"I've been on the 'Net. Listen, can you come get me? The story's about to break. It's all over the southern hemisphere already. It'll be on the morning news here in a few hours. Goddamned Miles. We figured he'd be the one to crack first."

"What? Kamla, what's going on?"

Cecilia is awake beside me, has turned on the bedside lamp. *Who?* she mouths. I make my lips mime a soundless "Kamla."

"It's a long story. Please, can you just come get me? You need to know about this. And I need another adult to talk to, someone who isn't my caretaker."

Another adult? "Okay, I'll be there soon." Kamla gives me the address and I hang up. I tell Cecilia what's going on; what I know, at least.

"You should just let her parents know that she's disturbed about something," she says. "Maybe it's another symptom of RGS."

"I'll talk to Babette and Sunil after Kamla tells me what's going on," I say. "I promised her to hear her out first."

"You sure that's wise? She's a child, Greg. She probably had a nightmare or something."

Feeding our child has made Cecilia's breasts sit lower on her rib cage. Her hips stretch at the nylon of her nightgown. Through the translucent fabric I can see the shadow of pubic hair and the valley that the curves of her thighs make. Her eyes are full of sleep, and her hair is a tousled mess, and she's so beautiful I could tumble her right now. But there's this frightened kid waiting to talk to me. I kiss Cecilia goodbye and promise to call her as soon as I've learned more.

Kamla's waiting for me outside the house. The night air is a little chilly, and she's a lonely, shivering silhouette against the front door. She makes to come in the passenger side of my car, but I motion her around to my side. "We're going to leave a note for your parents," I tell her. I brought one with me. "And we're just going sit right here in the car and talk."

"We can leave a note," she replies, "but we have to be away from here long enough so you can hear the whole story. I can't have Sunil and Babette charging to the rescue right now." I've never heard her call her parents by their first names; Bab and Sunil aren't into that kind of thing. Her face in her weirdly adult head looks calm, decisive. I find myself acquiescing. So I slip the note under the front door. It tells Babette and Sunil that Kamla's with me, that everything's all right. I leave them my cell phone number, though I know that Babette already has it.

Kamla gets into the car and closes the door quietly. We drive. I keep glancing over at her, but for a few minutes she doesn't say anything. I'm just about to ask her what was so urgent that she needed to pull a stunt like this when she says, "Your installation had a certain antique brio to it, Greg, really charming. My orig- . . . I mean, I have a colleague whose particular interest is in the nascent identity politics as expressed by artists of the twentieth and twenty-first centuries, and how that expression was the progenitor of current speciesism."

"Kamla, you been reading your mum's theory books?" I ask.

"No," she replied. There was so much bitterness in that one word. "I'm just a freak. Your kid's almost three, right?"

"Yeah."

"In a blink of an eye, barely a decade from now, his body will be entering puberty. He'll start getting erections, having sexual thoughts. . . ."

"I don't want to think about all that right now," I say. "I'm still too freaked that he's begun making poo-poo jokes. Kamla, is this the thing you wanted to tell me? Cause I'm not getting it."

"A decade from now, I'll have the body of a seven-year-old."

"You can't know that. There aren't any RGS kids who've reached their twenties yet."

"I know. I'm the oldest of them, by a few weeks." Another thing she can't know. "But Greg, we're all well past the age where normal children have achieved adolescence."

Goggling at her, I almost drove through a red light. I slammed on the brake. The car jolted to a halt. "What? What kind of shit is that? You're ten years old. A precocious ten, yes, but only ten, Kamla."

"Go in there." She points into the parking lot of a nearby grocery store. "It won't be open for another three hours."

I pull into the lot and park, leaving the engine running so we can have some heat in the car. "If the cops come by and see us," I say, "I could be in a lot of shit. They'll think I'm some degenerate Indian perv with a thing for little girls." Shit. I shouldn't be talking to a ten year old this way. Kamla always makes me forget. It's that big head, those big words.

"There's been very little sexual abuse of RGS people," she tells me. She says "people," not "children." "This" – she circles her face with her forefinger – "has none of the childish innocence that they crave. But we get beat up a lot by real children . . ."

"You *are* a real child!"

She glares at me, keeps going: ". . . who find us disconcerting to look at, and we get maltreated by adults for the same reason. Sunil and Babette are going to have to move soon. It's so hard for me to keep up this pretense, and I've managed to smart-mouth so much at school and in our neighborhood that it's become uncomfortable to live there any more."

My eyes have become accustomed enough to the dark that I can see the silent tears running down her cheeks. I want to hold her to me, to comfort her, but I'm afraid of how that will look if the cops show up. Besides, I'm getting the skin-crawly feeling that comes when you realise that someone with whom you've been making pleasant conversation is as mad as a hatter. "I'm taking you back home," I whisper. I start turning the key in the ignition.

"Please!" She puts a hand on my wrist. "Greg, please hear me out. I'll make it quick. I just don't know how to convince you."

I take my hand off the key. "Just tell me," I said. "Whatever it is, your parents love you. You can work it out."

She leaned back against the passenger side door and curled her knees up to her chest, a little ball of misery.

"Okay. Let me get it all out before you say anything else, all right?"

"All right."

"They grew us from cells from our originals; ten of us per original. They used a viral injection technique to alter our DNA; all of us have an extra-long tail on one of the strands of our DNA. Apart from longer telomeres to inhibit aging you need a lot of operons to drastically inhibit normal development."

The scientific jargon exiting smoothly from the mouth of a child could have been comic. But my skin was crawling. And I had goosebumps, too. She didn't appear to be repeating something she'd memorized.

"Each batch of ten yielded on average four viable blastocytes. They implanted those in womb donors; about two-thirds of them took. Most of those went to full term and were delivered. Had to be C-section, of course. Our huge heads presented too much of a risk for our birth mothers. We were usually about four years old before we were strong enough to lift our own heads. They treated us really well; best education, kept us fully informed from the start of what they wanted from us."

"Which was?" I whispered, terrified to hear the answer.

"Wait. You said you would." She continued her story. "Any of us could back out if we wanted to. Ours is a society that you would probably find strange, but we do have moral codes. Any of us who didn't want to make the journey could opt to undergo surgical procedures to correct some of the physical changes. Bones and muscles would lengthen, and they would reach puberty normally and thereafter age like regular people. They'll never achieve full adult height, and there'll always be something a little bit odd about their features, but it probably won't be so bad.

"About one-tenth of us were excited by the idea, the crazy, wonderful idea, and we decided to go through with it. They waited until we were age thirteen for us to confirm our decisions. In many cultures, that used to be the age when you were allowed to begin making adult decisions."

"You're ten, Kamla."

"I'm twenty-three, and my body won't start producing adult sex hormones for another fifty years. I won't attain my full growth till I'm ninety. I can expect. . . ."

"You're delusional," I whispered.

"I'm from your future," she says. God. The child's been watching too many B-movies. "It's too expensive to send an adult back, so they sent children instead. Clones of the originals, with their personalities superimposed onto our own. They sent back children who weren't children."

I'm starting up the car, I'm taking her back home right now. She needs help, therapy, or something. The sky is beginning to brighten. She doesn't try to stop me this time. Glumly, she goes on. "The weird thing is, even though this body isn't interested in adult sex, I remember what it was like, I remember enjoying it. It's those implanted memories from my original."

I'm edging past the speed limit in my hurry to get her back to her parents. I make myself slow down a little.

"Those of us living in extremely conservative countries are having a difficult time. We stay in touch by email, but not all of us have access to the technology. We've never been able to figure out what happened to

Kemi. Some of us were never adopted, had to make our own way as freakish children. So many lost. This fucking project better have been worth it."

I decide to keep her talking. "What project, Kamla?"

"Miles has talked. It's so hard to pretend you don't have an adult brain! Do you know what it's like turning in school work that's at a grade five level, when we've all written theses? We knew that one of us would crack, but we hoped it'd be later, when we'd all reached what your world would consider the age of majority."

We're cruising past a newspaper box. I look through its plastic window to see what the headline is. "I'M FROM THE FUTURE," SAYS BIG-HEADED BOY. Ah, one of our more erudite sources of journalism. Oh, christ. They all have this delusion, all the RGS kids. Crazily, I find myself wondering if Sunil and Bab can return Kamla to the adoption centre.

"We're becoming increasingly post-human," Kamla says. She's staring at the headline too. "Things change so quickly. Total upheaval of technology every five to eight years, difficult to keep up. Art helps us know how to think about change. Art has become very valuable to us."

"Thank heaven for that," I say. "Maybe in your world I could get paid a living wage for what I do."

She sits up in her seat and buckles herself in. Shit. I should have asked her to do that the minute she got in the car. I have one of those heart-in-the-mouth moments that I have often, now that I'm a parent. "You could get paid well," she agrees, "only not in ways you'd necessarily understand. And in my world, you'd be obsolete." She sniggers a little. "Video monitors! I'd never seen a brand new one, only mini-beams disguised to mimic ancient tech. We've all become anthropologists here in the past, as well as curators."

"What? You're a what?"

"I'm a curator, Greg. Our national gallery is having a giant retrospective; tens of thousands of works of art from all over the world, and all over the world's history. They sent us back to retrieve some of the pieces that had been destroyed. Expensive enough to send living biomaterial back; they couldn't afford to send us forward too, back to our time. So we're going to grow our way there. Those of us that survive."

There are more cars out on the road, more brakes squealing, more horns honking. "I'm not going to miss mass transit," she says. "Your world stinks, Greg."

Nothing I can say to that. We're nearly to her relatives' place. From my side, I lock her door. Of course she notices. She just glances at the sound. She looks like she's being taken to her death.

"I didn't know it until yesterday," she tells me, "but it was you I came for. That installation."

And now the too-clever bloody child has me where I live. Even though I know it's all air pie and Kamla is as nutty as a fruitcake, my heart's performing a tympanum of joy. The shell she found. It was me. "My installation's going to be in the retrospective?" I ask. Even as the words come out of my mouth, I'm embarrassed at how eager I sound, at how this little girl has dug her way into my psyche and found the thing which will make me respond to her.

She gasps and puts her hand to her mouth. "Oh, Greg! I'm so sorry; not you, the shell!"

My heart has suicided, the brief, hallucinatory hope dashed. "The shell?"

"Yes. In the culture where I live, speciesism has become a defining concept through which we understand what it means to be human, what it means to be an animal. Not every culture or sub-culture ascribes to it, but the art world of my culture certainly does." She's got her teacher voice on again. She does sound like a bloody curator.

"Human beings aren't the only ones who make art, Greg."

All right. Familiar territory. "Okay, perhaps. Bower birds make pretty bowers to catch a mate. Cetaceans sing to each other. But we're the only ones who make art mean; who make it comment on our everyday reality."

From the corner of my eye, I see her shake her ugly head. "No. We don't always know what they're saying. We can't always know the reality on which they're commenting. Who knows what a sea cucumber thinks of the conditions of its particular stretch of ocean floor?"

A sea cucumber? We've just turned onto her relatives' street. She'll be out of my hands soon. Poor Babette.

"Every shell is different," she says. My perverse brain instantly puts it to the tune of "Every Sperm is Sacred."

"Every shell is a life journal," Kamla continues, "made out of the very substance of its creator, and left as a record of what it thought. Sometimes interpretation is a trap, Greg. Sometimes we need to simply observe."

"And you've come all this way to take that . . . shell back?" I can see it sticking out of the chest pocket of her fleece shirt.

"I specialize in shell formations, or my original does. It's difficult to explain to you, because you don't have the concepts, and I don't have the time to teach you. But of its kind, this shell expresses a set of concepts that haven't been explored before by the artists of its species. After this one, all the others will draw on and riff off its conception of the world. They're the derivatives, but this is the original. In our world, it was lost."

Barmy. Loony. A nutter. "So how did you know that it even existed, then? Did the snail or slug that lived inside it take pictures, or something?" I've descended into cruelty. The child in me who can be hurt is still smarting that Kamla hasn't picked me, my work. I don't get to go to the future.

She gives me a wry smile, as though she understands. I pull up outside the house, start leaning on the horn. "The creature didn't take a picture, Greg," she says. "You did."

Fuck, fuck, fuck. With my precious video camera. It wasn't an interactive part of the exhibition, but I recorded every artifact with which I seeded the soil that went onto the gallery floor. I didn't tell her that. But she knew.

She nods. "Not all the tape survived, so we didn't know who had recorded it, or where the shell had come from. But we had an idea where the recording had come from."

Lights are coming on in the house. Kamla looks over there, sighs. "I haven't entirely convinced you, have I?"

"No," I say regretfully. But damn it, a part of me is not so sure.

"They're probably going to institutionalize me. All of us."

The door opens. Sunil is running out to the car, a gravid Babette following more slowly.

"You have to help me, Greg. Please? I'm going to outlive them all. I will get out. But in the meantime," she pulls the shell out of her pocket, offers it to me on her tiny palm, "please keep it safe for me?"

She opens the car door. "It's your ticket to the future," she says, and gets out of the car to greet her parents.

I lied. I fucking hate kids.

Laura Cottingham is currently working on a small book about Rainer Werner Fassbinder's 1973 film *Fear Eats the Soul* for the British Film Institute, forthcoming in the future currently known as 2005.

Nick Crowe is an artist based in Manchester, England. His first encounter with the science fiction genre took place during a two week period of hospitalization as a result of an acute appendicitis attack with intra-abdominal peritonitis. The book in question was a collection of short stories edited by Ray Bradbury. It has since been lost.

Aline Duriaud is a European video maker and writer based in New York City. She is currently editing her first feature length narrative digital video, and working on a screenplay.

Nalo Hopkinson is the internationally-acclaimed author of *Brown Girl in the Ring*, *Skin Folk*, and *Salt Roads*. Her books have been nominated for the Hugo, Nebula, Tiptree, and Philip K. Dick Awards; *Skin Folk* won a World Fantasy Award and the Sunburst Award. Born in Jamaica, Nalo moved to Canada when she was sixteen. She lives in Toronto.

Nico Israel lives in Brooklyn, New York. A literature professor and art critic, this is his first foray into fiction writing.

Matthew Licht is the author of *Ivy League Dick*, *The Ridiculous Avenger*, *Chicky Run*, *The Crazy-House Gag*. He lives in New York City.

Peter Maass is a contributing writer to the *New York Times Magazine* and the author of *Love Thy Neighbor: A Story of War.*

Rita McBride is an artist living and working in Cologne and New York. Her projects vary greatly from unorthodox books to very large sculptures. She is currently planning a sixty-meter tall carbon structure entitled *Mae West* to be erected in 2006 on the Effnerplatz in Munich.

Alexandre Melo is Portugal's foremost art critic, a professor of economics, and the world's greatest authority on spaghetti horor.

Glen Rubsamen is a painter primarily concerned with depicting situations of extreme emotional content in nature. His interest in writing the scientific romance novel stems from the personal belief that the world as we have been taught to perceive it is complete fiction. He lives and works in Cologne, Germany.

David Schafer is based in Los Angeles and teaches at the Art Center College of Design. Recent exhibitions include *Treble* in New York, and *ReModeling* at the UAM in Long Beach.

Mark von Schlegell divides his time between Los Angeles and Cologne, writing art criticism and science fiction, and teaching. His first SF novel, *Venusia*, will be released in November 2004 by Semiotext(e).

Rutger Wolfson studied Art and Cultural Sciences at the Erasmus University in Rotterdam and has been director of De Vleeshal, a center of contemporary art in Middelburg (NL) since 2000.

THE WAYS

Futureways is the second of four Ways books conceived by Rita McBride. The Ways books – entitled *Heartways*, *Futureways*, *Crimeways*, and *Myways* – exploit and decipher genre writing with an entertaining and refreshing collective structure. The books include contributions from more than fifty artists, architects, writers, journalists, curators, and critics.

Heartways: The Exploits of Genny O
edited by Rita McBride & Erin Cosgrove
NOW AVAILABLE

Futureways
edited by Rita McBride & Glen Rubsamen

Crimeways
edited by Rita McBride & Matthew Licht
AVAILABLE IN 2005

Myways
edited by Rita McBride & David Gray
AVAILABLE IN 2005